Her Dangerous Lover

KRISTIN M GLENN

All rights reserved.
Copyright © 2023 Kristin M Glenn

No part of this book may be used or reproduced by any means, graphic, electronic, or mechanical, including photocopying, recording, taping or by any information storage retrieval system without the written permission of the author except in the case of brief quotations embodied in critical articles and reviews.

Because of the dynamic nature of the Internet, any web addresses or links contained in this book may have changed since publication and may no longer be valid. The views expressed in this work are solely those of the author and do not necessarily reflect the views of the publisher, and the publisher hereby disclaims any responsibility for them.

ISBN: 979-8-88945-176-1 (paperback)
ISBN: 979-8-88945-178-5 (hardback)
eISBN: 979-8-88945-177-8

Brilliant Books Literary
137 Forest Park Lane Thomasville
North Carolina 27360 USA

Printed in the United States of America

Chapter 1

He got up from the bed, and looked at her with desire in his eyes. He had just made love to the most beautiful women he had ever laid eyes on, and she was his wife. John and Shaila Anderson were the perfect couple, and they had the perfect life. They had been married nearly nine years. John Patrick Anderson was born into a very prestigious, respectable, and wealthy family. The Andersons had made millions in real estate throughout the years. Although John was born into wealth, he had made quite a fortune of his own. At forty years old, he was a Pediatric Cardiologist, one of the best in his field. John was very easy on the eyes. He stood six feet six inches tall, weighing about 275 lbs of pure muscle. He was blessed with dark chocolate skin, dark brown eyes you could get lost in. He was that fine.

"Why are you staring at me like that? You know we don't have time for another round." Shaila smirked, giving him a nice sensual kiss.

"My beautiful wife lying next to me. I never tire of looking at your gorgeous body, or making love to you."

John looked at her with some serious bedroom eyes. "I wish I could stay in bed and make love to you all day, but my patients need me," John said with regret.

"I know, me too, but I have a new client I have to meet with today," Shaila said.

"Really, who is it?? John asked, intrigued.

"Marc Wilson."

"Marc Wilson, as in Wilson Inc,?" John asked with astonishment.

"He's the one. If I play my card right, he may just contract with our firm to represent his company exclusively."

"Very impressive, sweetheart. You'll have him eating out of the palm of your hands. He would be crazy not to contract with your firm," he said lovingly.

"Thank you, honey. I really needed to hear that.

She got out of bed and headed across their huge master bedroom into their master bathroom. She really wanted to take a long hot bath, but she didn't have the time. She was already running late due to the early morning lovemaking she had with her handsome husband. Shaila was a strikingly beautiful woman. At thirty eight years old, she stood five feet ten inches with gorgeous golden brown skin, long brown hair flowing down her back and hazel eyes. There was not an ounce of fat anywhere on her body. She took great care of herself by working out and eating right. She and John were health fanatics to the core, and although they had their indulgences like chocolate and ice cream, they very rarely engaged in eating them. Shaila was a partner in one of the most prestigious law firms in the country, York, Anderson, and Locke. Shaila came from a long line of attorneys. Going all the way back to her great grandfather. Both her parents were attorneys now retired and living in Indiana, Paul and Christine Meadows were always on the go and they loved it. They adored their children. Greg was the oldest at forty two. Thomas was in the middle at forty. Then came Shaila, the baby. Shaila was spoiled rotten, and she was a daddy's girl. She couldn't do anything wrong in his eyes. Her mother and her brothers also adored her. She was a genius when it came to her work. Nobody could touch her, especially when it came to corporate law. It was her area of expertise.

Shaila stepped into the shower and showered quickly. She got out and started to get herself ready for her big meeting with Marc

Wilson. Of all the days to be running late, she thought to herself while drying off.

"Honey, I'm going to be late coming home from the hospital tonight. I have a meeting with Jerry this evening at five o'clock," John called to her while in the bedroom.

Jerry Smith was the Chief of Staff at Mercy Hospital. Jerry was also a surgeon, and a very good friend to Shaila and John.

"Ok," she said while putting on her makeup. "Tell Jerry I said hi."

John came up behind her and put his arms around her tiny waist. "I will be sure to tell him." He caressed her breast with his hands, and kissed her neck. Chills went straight through her making her groan and breathe heavily."

"You keep this up and we'll never make it to work," she said with a smile. "You better get yourself in that shower before I take advantage of this situation," She said, laughing.

"I'm going. I'm going. You are just so beautiful. It's hard to keep my hands off you."

Chapter 2

John pulled into his private parking spot at Mercy Hospital in his jet black Mercedes SL 600. Making his way into the hospital, he headed to the nursing station.

"Good morning Dr. Anderson," one of the nurses said.

"Good morning, Alice. I'm here to make my rounds. Anything earth shattering I should know about?" He questioned.

"Nothing earth shattering. Although Cindy Cramer has been asking about her favorite doctor. I think she might have a crush on you, be careful," she said, jokingly.

"Oh I think I can handle it," he said, while laughing.

"How's my favorite patient?" John asked as he stepped into Cindy's hospital room.

"I'm fine. I'm just watching television with mommy."

"Hello, Dr. Anderson," Jennifer Cramer said.

"Good morning Jennifer,"

"Are you ready to go home?" Looking at the five year old little girl.

"Yes, I really want to go home. Can I go home today…please?" Cindy pleaded.

"Well, let's see. It looks like you are doing extremely well after surgery. I'm very impressed with your progress. I just need to examine you to make sure everything is going smoothly," she said with a caring attitude.

Cindy Cramer had heart surgery due to a hole in her heart since birth. After careful consideration and discussions with other specialists, Mr. and Mrs. Cramer along with Dr. Anderson, decided it would be in her best interest to repair the heart now opposed to later on down the road. She had been in the hospital for a week to make sure her heart was in tiptop condition after surgery.

The day before John had ordered an EKG, an echocardiogram, and a chest x ray. He had the films with him when he came into the room. He had to check out everything, and the films all looked good. There were no signs of any abnormalities. Now he had to check her oxygen saturation level. If that checked out all right, she would be ready to go home. The oxygen level was where it needed to be. John concluded the little girl was doing extremely well. All her vitals were excellent and her heart rhythm was beating smoothly.

"Well, it looks like you are going to get your wish. You can go home today. I will get your discharge papers ready," John said with excitement.

"Yeah!" Jennifer and Cindy screamed.

"I can finally take my baby home? Thank you so much."

"You're welcome. I will need to see her back in my office in one week for a follow up."

"She'll be there. Thank You for everything you did for my little girl. You saved her life. I will always be grateful to you."

"I'm just glad I could help that beautiful little girl. I'll see you all next week," he said, shaking her hand then walking out the door.

After making his morning rounds and finishing up his charting, John went outside to the lunch area to take in the beautiful scenery and to call Shaila to see how she was doing.

"Shaila Anderson," she said, answering her cell phone.

"Hello, sweetheart. How's my baby doing?"

"I'm doing fine now that I hear your voice."

"Have you had your meeting with Marc Wilson yet?" He asked, inquisitively.

"No, not yet. We're meeting for lunch at Antonio's at one o'clock. I'm kind of nervous."

"Don't be. You are going to knock him off his feet. That I guarantee."

"You always know how to make me feel so much better. You always say the right things."

"I love you, sweetheart," he said, lovingly.

"I love you, too," she whispered back to him as she hung up the phone.

Shaila sat at her massive mahogany desk looking out the window wondering how her meeting with Marc Wilson was going to fare. Looking around her office, she had an incredible picture window overlooking Central Park. Hanging on her walls were exquisite pictures of African American art, which she and John had bought at an art auction just for her office. To the right of her desk sat an ebony leather sofa so enticing you could easily take a nap. On her desk sat her laptop computer, a desk calendar and several pictures of John and her family, including her nieces and nephews whom she adored immensely. She and John talked about having kids, but they had been really busy with their careers. Right now she was content spoiling her brother's kids.

"I see you're in deep thought sitting in here," Sara said, standing in the doorway.

Sara Jones was a stunning blonde woman who had just gotten out of law school and passed the bar about two years ago. She was twenty eight years old and had everything going for her. She was an ambitious, determined young lady. She stood about five feet nine inches tall with shoulder length blond hair and blue eyes that looked like crystal blue waters. Shaila took Sara under her wing when she was first hired. She helped Shaila with research and depositions on many cases she worked on. Shaila taught her how to be aggressive when it was merited and passive when it was essential, especially in the courtroom. Sara was becoming a very experienced litigator. Shaila always told her she was going to be a top-notch attorney some day. Sara had always looked up to Shaila. She was her mentor and her friend. Sara proved to be smart, hard working, and loyal. Shaila really trusted her.

"Hey Sara, what's going on?"

"Just doing some research on a case for Luke. What about you? Is everything ok?" You seem distracted."

"No, I'm fine. Just thinking. I have a meeting with Marc Wilson today at one o'clock. I'm just a little nervous I guess.'

"Why? You've handled multi-million dollar clients with such ease in the past, why is this any different?"

"Because we dated years ago in college before I met John. I haven't seen him in years. I'm not sure what to expect."

"You are kidding, right?" Sara inquired.

"No. I'm not kidding. Not in the least. The bad thing about it is John doesn't know I dated him in college. I never told him."

"Why not tell him? Why all the secrecy? John had to know you dated other people before you started dating him, right?"

"I don't know. It just never came up I guess. John never asked about my past relationships, and I never really asked about his. Besides, that was a long time ago."

"Did you love him?" Sara asked with curiosity.

"Yes, I did. I love him so much it nearly killed me when we broke up."

"May I ask why you two broke up? If I'm being too personal please tell me."

"No. I don't mind you asking me. He cheated on me with my roommate, my best friend."

"Shaila, I'm sorry. That must have hurt like hell. He cheated with her best friend? Now that is unforgivable," Sara said with disdainment.

"I broke it off." Shaila started to explain. "He tried to get me back, but I wasn't having any of that. He called me everyday for three weeks telling me he loved me, he made a terrible mistake, and how he would do anything to get me back. Please give him another chance. You know the drill. All the BS came pouring out when he found out he was busted bigger than life. I told him I wasn't going to take him back and to leave me alone. I didn't trust him. He had broken my heart, and I would never forgive him. Shortly after that, I met John and that was that."

"Do you think he wants to meet with you to try to get you back?" Sara asked.

"Surely not. He knows I'm happily married. I'm sure this is just business. Besides, he's probably married with a family now," Shaila said.

"I don't know. He has been all over the internet here lately. He had just made another one hundred million in some kind of oil venture, and it didn't mention anything about a family or him being married," Sara said.

"Did you ever stop to think he might want to meet with me because I'm a damn good attorney? I'm good at what I do, not to mention this is one of the best law firms in the country. He could do a lot worse than contracting with us," she explained with a sigh.

"I'm not saying that you aren't good. Everybody knows you are a brilliant attorney. All I'm saying is he might have an ulterior motive. By the way, did he specifically ask to meet you?"

"No, he didn't. Ben thought I should take the meeting because this is my field and I'm good with 'putting on the charm' as he put it.

"I have a feeling you aren't going to have a problem reeling him in. The question is when you do land him as a client, are you going to be able to handle it?" Sara asked with concern.

"Of course, I can handle it. This is business and nothing personal. I am not the least bit interested in Marc Wilson. I love my husband."

"I know you do. John is a great guy, and you two are a match made in heaven. I just hope Marc respects that and doesn't try to screw up your marriage. He might just want back what he lost years ago," Sara said with warning.

"If you need anything please let me know and be careful will you?" "I will, Thanks Sara."

Sara turned and walked out the door.

Chapter 3

Antonio's was a beautiful Italian restaurant with just the right atmosphere, not to mention the wonderful food they served. Shaila pulled up to the valet in her Mercedes SUV and parked. The valet opened her door, and when she got out, the valet gave her a ticket and proceeded into the driver's seat.

"Hello Mrs. Anderson, it's nice to see you again," the valet said with a smile.

"Hello Eric, it's good to see you too," Shaila said back.

Shaila knew almost everyone by name who worked there. This was one of her favorite restaurants and the staff loved her because she was very nice and she tipped very well.

"Mrs. Anderson, it's so good to see you again," the hostess said.

"Thank you, it's good to see you," Shaila smiled. "I'm meeting Marc Wilson at one o'clock. Is he here?"

"Yes, he is. Right this way."

Shaila followed the hostess to a table by the window. Standing there was a six foot five inch tall man with light brown skin and green eyes. His hair was a short cut that complimented his head. He was even more gorgeous than when he was in college. He wore a navy blue Gucci suit, a red Gucci tie and a pair of navy blue Gucci shoes. His suit looked like it was tailor made to fit, and he looked like a million bucks. Marc had some steamy affairs in his past, but none of them had ever panned out. He was still very much in love with Shaila even after all these years. Nobody could compare to Shaila, although she didn't know that.

"Shaila, it's good to see you again. You look even more beautiful now than in college." Marc said with a smile.

Shaila wore a Versace hunter green skirt suit with matching pumps, and a Versace bag to match. Her hair was up in a French twist that completely complimented her face. She was wearing a diamond heart necklace and a gold rolex watch John had given her for her birthday last year. She oozed class and professionalism.

The waitress came over and took their drink orders. Shaila ordered an iced tea and Marc ordered a gin and tonic.

"How have you been, Mark? From what I've read in the papers, you are doing quite well for yourself." Shaila said, nonchalantly.

"I'm doing ok. I've been blessed. I can say that much," he said with a grin. "How's everything with you? Everything is going well I hope.

"Everything is going well, thank you for asking."

Just then the waitress came back with their drinks. "Are you ready to order?" The waitress asked.

"Yes, I'll have the fettuccini alfredo please, thank you," Shaila said with a smile.

"I'll have the same, thank you," Marc added.

The waitress wrote down their orders and walked away.

"I heard you got married to John Anderson. Isn't he some kind of Doctor now?"

"Yes, he's a Pediatric Cardiologist. We have been married for nearly nine years now."

"I've read about some of the real estate holdings his family has acquired just in the past couple of years, very impressive."

"Well, the Andersons are very impressive people, not to mention very nice."

"Well, I'm glad you are happy," Marc said.

"I am very happy."

"Listen Shaila, I never got to say how sorry I was for sleeping with Brooke and for hurting you so badly in college. I was an idiot. I didn't know how much I loved you until I lost you. I hope you can forgive me for what I did to you," Marc said sadly.

"It doesn't matter. It happened so long ago. I got over it and moved on. Let's just forget about it, ok?"

"Do you still hate me?"

"I never hated you, Marc. I was hurt. I did love you at one time, but like I said that was a long time ago. Let's not talk about this anymore. What's done is done. You can't change the past," Shaila said.

"You're right," Marc agreed.

During lunch, Shaila used her charm and professionalism to make her point about how it would be beneficial to everyone involved for Wilson, Inc. to contract with York, Anderson, and Locke exclusively. Marc was so impressed with what she had to say that he signed the contract right there on the spot. Even though he had already made up his mind before he met Shaila for lunch, he was still quite impressed with her expertise and professionalism on the matter. The lunch, however, was just a formality, just a way to feel her out to see where he stood. He would do whatever it took to get Shaila back. Shaila was the one he wanted and he would do anything to make sure that happened.

"Fore!" John yelled after teeing the golf ball three hundred yards to the next hole.

"You make me sick the way you hit that ball like that. You should have been a professional golfer," Malcolm Parker said.

Malcolm was a nice looking man in his fifties. His hair was gray and balding, but back in the day it was blonde. He had a very nice way about him. He was a genuinely nice person to everyone he came in contact with, even though he was vulgar sometimes and he did cheat on his wife, he was a good friend. He was an ob/gyn and loved his work. He loved to deliver babies, not to mention the women who had the babies.

"How's that beautiful wife of yours," Malcolm asked.

"She's doing very well. She's something isn't she?"

"You're a very lucky man."

"Thanks, um, so are you," John said, unconvincingly.

"Please. Let's tell the truth shall we. Maria is a first class witch. She gets on my nerves so bad, I'd like to kick her into the next hemisphere." Malcolm said, smiling.

"Then why do you put up with her? Why not get a divorce if it's that bad at home?"

"Please and have her take everything I have? Are you crazy? Besides, I get what I want on the side. I got some good loving going on and the best part is I don't have to beg for it."

"You are a nasty old man cheating on Maria like that," John said.

"Oh come on now, don't tell me you never thought about getting into another woman's pants other than Shaila."

"Shaila means everything to me. I would never cheat on her. Besides, if I did, and she found out, you could kiss my ass goodbye, and I do mean literally."

"I tell you, if I had Shaila to go home, I wouldn't stray.

"Please, who are you trying to fool? This is me you're talking to. You know it's in your blood. You like the danger of it all. I'm telling you man to man you better be careful messing with all these women you could get yourself into some serious trouble. Women don't like to be played. I haven't even mentioned their husbands. They won't hesitate to put a hot one in your ass real quick for messing around with their wives. And what about all the diseases that are out there in this world? I could go on and on. I hope you are at least using protection," John said with concern and warning.

"I got it covered, Don't you worry about me. I never do anything without my jimmy hat. Besides, if I do go, at least I'll go doing what I do best, sexing a woman," Malcolm said with a grin.

Laughing out loud, John said," You are a trifling old man. All I'm saying is watch your back."

"Dr. John Anderson," he said, answering his ringing cell phone.

"Hi baby," Shaila said to him. "Where are you?"

"Hey sweetie, I'm on the golf course with Dr. Porter. We're getting a few holes in before my meeting with Dr. Smith.

"Really, well tell Malolm don't be getting my man into any mess out there." Shaila said with a laugh. "Guess what, I got Marc Wilson to sign a contract with us today. He signed right after lunch today. Can you believe that, baby? His business is contracted exclusively with our firm. Everyone here is so excited. That is a lot of money coming in for our firm," She said with excitement and apprehension.

"Congratulations sweetie. I am so proud of you. I knew you could do it. I never had a doubt in my mind. We need to celebrate when I get home. I should be home around seven."

"Ok, I'll see you then. I love you," said Shaila.

"I love you too, bye sweetie."

Chapter 4

"Hi Sidney," Shaila said to her secretary as she walked into her office.

"Any messages?"

"Just the usual sitting on your desk.

"Thanks."

Congratulations on your new client. Oh, there were flowers delivered to you about ten minutes ago. They are gorgeous. I am so jealous. I never get flowers sent to me," Sidney said, while laughing.

"Well, then, I'll have to send you some. Who are the flowers from?"

"I don't know. There was a card inside the bouquet though. Maybe John sent them to you to say I love you and congratulations."

Sidney had worked for Shaila for almost four years now. Shaila really depended on her. Sidney was her rock. If Shaila ever got bogged down and couldn't get something done or didn't have time to take lunch, Sidney always had her back. She would get her lunch and stay late to help her if she needed, although Shaila very rarely asked her to do so. Sidney did what she needed to do without having to be told. That was what Shaila loved about her.

Sitting on top of her desk were twelve sterling silver roses in a crystal vase. The card read: *Thank you for a wonderful lunch. It was good seeing you again. I look forward to working with you. Always Marc.*

Knocking on her door stood an older man in his early fifties with wavy salt and pepper hair, caramel skin, and brown eyes. Benjamin York was fifty five, but looked like he was forty. He was a handsome man who commanded respect. He was a tiger in the courtroom like Shaquille O'Neal worked the basketball court. He was that good if not better. He was the senior partner in the firm. He intimidated everyone in the firm, everyone but Shaila. She knew what a pussycat cat he really was because she had worked with him for so many years.

"Hey Shaila, I heard congratulations are in order. You landed the Wilson account. That is why I sent you. You could charm a dog away from a meaty bone," Ben said with a laugh.

"You're crazy, Ben. Thank you," she said, laughing.

"Nice flowers. Did you and hubby have a fight? Does he need to make amends for something?"

"No, no fights between John and me. We're fine. Thank you for your concern," She said with sarcasm. "They are actually from Marc Wilson. He sent them to say thank you."

"Damn woman, what exactly happened between you two at lunch? You must have impressed the hell out of him for him to send you flowers like that. I know you showed him a little leg, didn't you?"

"Shut up," she said with a laugh.

"You know I'm playing with you girl. On the serious tip, you are that good. I'll see you later."

"Bye," She said as he walked out the door.

"I'm beginning to think I made a huge mistake getting involved with Marc again even if it is in a professional capacity," Shaila whispered to herself.

"Shaila Anderson," she said, picking up her ringing office phone.

"I was just wondering if you got the roses I sent you," Marc asked.

"Yes I did. They are beautiful, thank you. You remembered I love sterling silver roses. What did I do to deserve this?"

"Think of it as an I'm sorry can we be friends again gift."

"But I already told you all is forgiven. You didn't have to do this."

"I know you did. I just felt you deserved them, that's all."

"You take care, Shaila. I will talk to you soon."
"I will. You do the same."

John walked into the Manhattan penthouse to find a trail of sterling silver rose petals leading upstairs to the master bedroom. He put his medical bag in the foyer and proceeded upstairs. He opened the door to the bedroom to find candles lit all over the bedroom. Sitting on a table in the middle of the bedroom was lobster, steamed vegetables, champagne chilling in a bucket of ice, and chocolate mousse pie for dessert. Shaila came out wearing a form-fitted navy blue strapless sheath dress with a slit that went up to her thigh.

"Damn, what did I do to deserve all of this?" John asked, looking at his gorgeous wife. "You look stunning, but I have a feeling you aren't going to be in that dress for too much longer if I have my way."

"I just missed you, that's all I wanted to do something special for my husband. Besides, you said we were going to celebrate tonight."

John grabbed her and pulled her to him. He kissed her with all the passion he could muster. Groaning with delight, Shaila leaned into him waiting for him to take her. He picked her up into his arms and carried her to the California king-sized bed. He laid her on top of the bed and proceeded to kiss her again. His tongue touched and caressed hers all the time she moaned with pleasure. He stood up and began taking his shirt off. He revealed his rippled six-pack abs. He unbuckled his pants and slowly took them off giving her a sexy dance. He stood there looking at her ready to ravage her. His manhood throbbed in front of her. He moved to her and started taking off her dress. He gently slid her dress down over her hips pushing her dress the rest of the way to the floor. He kissed her neck down to her breasts. He paused for a second before he took her nipple into his mouth caressing it with his tongue. She moaned in the heat of passion. He kissed her stomach down her thigh. He licked her right leg up to her thigh until he reached her lips. He kissed her passionately. His tongue was domineering and enticing. He proceeded to lick down her stomach until he reached between her legs. He licked and teased her clit. She wanted him so badly she ached for him to be inside her. He teased her clit with his tongue putting her into a passion induced coma.

"Oh baby, please don't tease me like this," she said heavily. He began tasting her insides like a sea of champagne flowing inside and he was drunk on her taste. She lurched herself up arching her back to get the full effect of his tongue inside her. She grabbed hold of the sheets. Her eyes rolled back into her head and she let out a yelp that would wake King Tut.

"I'm not done with you yet," he said, kissing every inch of her body from front to back teasing, exploring, and tasting every single inch. Tonight was her night. This was all about pleasuring her and he was definitely fulfilling this task. He kissed her neck and her stomach. He took her hands into his own and brought her up into him with her legs straddling his hips. With hips rocking back and forth, he slowly entered her, thrusting slowly at first faster and faster to where he was ready to explode, but he was waiting for her to reach her peak. She moaned heavily and with so much passion she finally screamed out his name.

"Oh John, yes, yes, yes!" She screamed. After her release, everything that was pent up inside him bubbled to the surface causing him to jerk and scream like Tarzan exploding inside her like a thunderbolt. Lying on her side looking into those brown eyes she said, "baby, what you do to me is beyond words. I love you so much."

"Baby, all I want to do is to please you," he said lustfully.

"Well you achieved your goal because I have been immensely pleasured. Are you hungry? We do have all that food over there sitting and wasting away."

"I'm not really all that hungry at the moment, are you?"

"Nope."

"Well, what should we do?" He asked.

"I know we'll think of something."

He leaned and kissed her and they made love all night and into the morning leaving the food sitting in the middle of the bedroom.

Chapter 5

Nothing could prepare Marc for the passion he felt for Shaila even after all of those years. He knew he still had some feelings for her, but he didn't know how much until he saw her at Antonio's. He was still totally in love with this woman. Sitting in his high rise office he couldn't get any work done. He kept thinking about Shaila. "I have to get this woman out of my mind if I'm going to get any work done," he said to himself.

With the contract Marc signed the day before in his hand, Jeff dropped them on Marc's desk. Jeff was Marc's business partner and friend. "Please tell me you didn't sign this contract. Have you lost your mind?" He asked, shaking his head in disbelief. "I think you are making a big mistake by contracting with York, Anderson, and Locke. You're setting yourself up for a serious fall if you ask me."

"Maybe I am, but they are the best firm in the country. They have a great reputation. We need that.

"I understand all of that, but why Shaila's particular firm? There are plenty of other firms out there that have very reputable attorneys,"

"Because they are the best," Marc shot back.

Jeff let out a deep breath and sighed. "I hope you know what you're doing. Do you really think she will leave her husband for you?

You know she is a very honorable woman. She wouldn't do that," Jeff pleaded.

"I want her back plain and simple, I have no intention of letting her slip away this time."

"That's my point. She's not yours to let slip away. She's MARRIED! You seem to be forgetting that fact. You need to let this go. This is not healthy. You need to find someone else and settle down and put Shaila out of your mind."

"With who? It's not that simple," he said, throwing his pen on top of the paper on his desk. "Every woman I have dated in the past wanted my money and nothing else. I know Shaila is not like that. She has her own money. She sure as hell doesn't need mine. Not only that, I have never stopped loving her. That oughta count for something, right"

"Is that why you want Shaila because you know she won't go after your bank account?"

No, that's not it at all. Hear what I'm saying, I LOVE HER!"

"Man, talking to you is like talking to a brick wall. You are so determined to mess up your life by pining for a married woman."

"I'm not messing up anything. I was with her first. John was just a rebound thing. I will show her I'm the one she really wants."

"Would you listen to yourself? You sound like a child 'I had her first.' Reiterating what Marc had just said to make his point. "You talk about her like she's an object. She isn't. She's a human being," he said angrily.

"Damn man, will you stop hatin on me? I know she's a human being. I don't think of her as an object."

Shaking his head, Jeff said, "ok man, don't say I didn't warn you." Jeff walked out of his office.

Sitting alone in his office, Marc thought of nothing but Shaila. His every thought was of her. The way she walked. The way she smiled. The way she looked. He was undeniably obsessed with her. He couldn't help his feelings. How was he going to make Shaila see they belonged together? He had to win her back, but how? Seducing her was not the ticket. He knew he couldn't do that because she was way too smart to fall for something like that. Jeff was right. She wasn't going to leave her husband. He had to figure out a way to get John out of the picture, then he would have Shaila all to himself. He would devise a plan and put it into action. He picked up the phone and dialed a number.

"Hello," a female voice answered.

"It's me," Marc said. "I need you to do me a favor.

"Anything for you, baby. What's up?"

"Here's what I need you to do." He went into detail of what he wanted her to do and how he wanted it done. She complied and told him she would get right on it. They hung up the phone. He sat back in his seat with a big fat grin on his face.

Chapter 6

John sat at the breakfast table reading the paper when Shaila walked in the room. She came up behind and put her arms around him and kissed the back of his neck.

"Hey baby," he said to her. "You look rested. I was going to wake you up, but you looked so peaceful lying there, I couldn't do it."

"I needed the rest. The way you put it on me last night and this morning tired me out," she said with a smirk. "I'm going to miss you so much while you're away."

"I'm going to miss you too, baby. If I didn't have to go I wouldn't, but I have to go. I'm speaking at a seminar. I wish you could come with me. I love when you come to seminars with me," he said, caressing her cheek.

"I wish I could go too, but I have to be here to finalize the documents for the Wilson account. I'm the one who got him to sign the contract. It would be unprofessional to throw it into someone else's lap.

"I know, and I understand. I'll only be gone for three days anyway. It won't be that bad."

"What time is your flight?"

"Three."

"Do you want me to drive you to the airport?"

"No, that's ok. I have a driver. Besides, I can't bear to say goodbye to you at the airport. I'd rather do that here."

"Are you all packed?"

"Yes."

"Well I better get ready to go to the office," she said. "You will call me as soon as you get checked into your hotel, won't you."

"You know I will. I will call you everyday. I promise."

She went upstairs and put on her clothes to go to work. "I'm gone, sweetie," she said. Taking the paper out of his hand, sitting on his lap, and giving him a sensual kiss. "I love you, John. You have a safe trip."

"I love you, too."

The airport was a complete madhouse. People were everywhere. Ever since the 9/11 tragedy, security was unbelievably tight. They had scanned John's bags three times in an hour. It seemed everywhere he went someone scanned him or his bag. He wasn't the only one though. Everyone was being scanned two or three times. He finally made it to his terminal with an hour to spare. He checked in his bags and picked up his ticket. He sat down and started reading his medical journal he had brought with him. Standing next to him was a pretty young woman probably in her late twenties.

"Is this seat taken?" She asked.

"No, please have a seat," John said.

"I'm Cheryl."

"John."

"Well, John, It's nice to meet you."

"You too."

"Are you on your way to Boston for business or pleasure?" She asked.

'Business. I'm speaking at a seminar."

A seminar, huh" What do you do?"

"I'm a Pediatric Cardiologist."

"Very impressive. You save the lives of children. I love that. How long have you been a surgeon?"

"Almost ten years. What about you? What do you do?"

"I'm a real estate agent. I'm going to Boston to try and lock in a potential buyer on a home on the the market."

"Really? My family is in real estate."

"What a small world. Who's your family?"

"Anderson Realty."

"You're kidding. Your father is James Anderson? As in the James Anderson, he's a legend. I read about him on social media recently. He just sold the Beltmore Hotel for fifty million."

"Yes, that's him."

For the next hour John and Cheryl talked about their careers and family. John told her all about Shaila and what she did for a living and how great she was. She told him she was married once, but now she was divorced. Her career had gotten in the way of her marriage and her husband couldn't handle her making more money than him. They talked until it was time to board the plane. They said their goodbyes and boarded the plane separately.

Shaila sat in her office going over the documents for the Wilson account. She had to make sure everything was in order. Marc was going to be there soon to finalize the contract. Although she was happy the firm landed this lucrative account, she was also apprehensive about it. Something was gnawing at her in the back of her mind, but she couldn't figure out what it was. It wasn't that she had any feelings for Marc. That had been over for a long time. She was interested in him for business reasons only. It was clear he was only interested in business also, so what was the problem? Why was she making a mountain out of a molehill? "I'm thinking too much," she thought to herself.

The buzzer in her office interrupted her thoughts. It was Sidney telling her Marc was there to go over the fine print of the contract. Shaila told her to send him in.

"Hi Marc, it's good to see you again. I have the rest of the contract ready for you to sign. Would you like me to explain anything before you sign?"

"No, thank you. I understand everything quite clearly. Besides, I trust you. I don't think you would try and mess me over.

"Well then just sign here."

He did as he was told, and handed her back the contract. Shaila then asked Sidney to make copies to give to Marc for his files. While Sidney made copies, Marc and Shaila talked about what was going on in their lives. He told her about the deal he had just made and how his company was becoming internationally known. He talked about his relationships and how they never lasted because he wasn't ready to settle down, or he couldn't find the right woman. He had to be careful with who he got involved with because his money was a big issue in a relationship. He was a multi-billionaire who was listed on the internet number seven as the world's richest men and every woman he met knew it. He didn't know who he could trust, and Shaila felt sorry for him. He deserved someone who would love him for him not his bank account. In the middle of their conversation, Sidney came back with the copies and handed the originals back to Shaila and the copies to Marc.

"Thank you, Sidney," Shaila said.

"It's five o'clock, I'm going to head home unless you need me to do anything else for you before I leave," Sidny said.

"No, you go home to that handsome husband of yours. I'll see you tomorrow. It was nice meeting you, Mr. Wilson. I hope to see you again soon," Sidney said.

"The pleasure was all mine," Marc said back, and with that, Sidney turned and walked out the door.

"So I guess you're going to head home to that lucky husband of yours?"

"John is out of town on business. He's speaking at a seminar in Boston. I'll probably get some take out and go home and curl up with a good book.

"Well, since John is out of town, would you do me the honor of going out to dinner with me? Just for old times sake. It's nothing fancy. Just dinner between two old friends. What do you think?"

"I don't think that's a good idea. I don't mix business with pleasure."

"Come on, what's the harm? Unless you think you might want to do more than have dinner."

"You're right. What's the harm in a little dinner between friends," she relented.

She got up, grabbed her purse from the drawer, and with Marc following, proceeded to walk out of the office.

They had dinner at a quaint little French restaurant called La Maison. Both Marc and Shaila were fluent in French, so most of their conversation was in French. After about an hour of talking and laughing about old times, Marc brought up the trip they took to Cancun while they were in college.

"Do you remember how much fun we had? I will never forget that trip. I still have very fond memories even after all of these years,"

"How could I forget? We were something back then. Everything seemed so right. We were so carefree. We didn't care about anything but being together. We just knew we were going to stay together, didn't we? We were so naive and stupid. I guess things really do change."

"Yes, I guess they do," he said in a somber mood. Trying to lighten the mood he asked, " hey do you remember the night we went down to the beach? It was a little after three in the morning. There was no one around and we ended up making love in the sand right there on the beach? Do you remember that? You were so scared someone was going to see us. You kept looking everywhere but at me," he said with a huge laugh. "You looked so beautiful under that moonlit sky. It was at that moment I knew I loved you."

She put her hands over her face to hide her embarrassment. "What the hell were we thinking?" She asked, putting her hands back down on the table. "I was so sure we were going to be arrested for illicit behavior or something. Can you imagine what could have happened?" She asked with a chuckle. "God, we were so stupid and careless."

Just at that moment they both reached for the sugar to out in their coffee. Marc placed his hand on top of hers. She let out a deep breath and eased her hand out from under his. They could feel the intense moment they just shared. Something was happening. He looked straight into her eyes and smiled. She smiled back at him.

"That seems like a lifetime ago. We have changed a lot since we were in college," she ran her fingers through her long flowing hair and flipped it to one side. He looked at her in such a way he had to close his eyes to break the intensity between them.

"It's time for me to get home now. I have an early morning tomorrow," she said. "Thanks for dinner.

"It was my pleasure. I enjoyed your company. Please don't be a stranger. Give me a call sometime. Maybe we can do this again."

"Yeah, maybe we can."

He paid the bill and left a generous tip. They got up and he walked her to her car. He kissed her on the cheek and put her in the car. He shut her door and waved her off.

Chapter 7

John got settled into his hotel room looking over his itinerary of seminars he had to speak at. He took off his tie and unbuttoned his shirt. He was about to get comfortable and take a shower when there was a knock on the door. He went to open the door and was surprised to see Cheryl standing on the other side of the door.

"Cheryl, what are you doing here? How did you find me?" He asked surprised.

"Don't be upset with me, but I followed you here. I don't know anyone here and I thought you and I could hang out and see the sights together. We had such a connection while we were talking earlier. I wanted to keep engaging in the company.

"I don't think that's a good idea. Besides, I'm only going to be here for three days and I'm going to be very busy until I leave for New York. I won't have time for any sightseeing."

"I think I'm being too subtle" She threw her arms around his neck and kissed him on his lips and his neck. "I want you. I've wanted you ever since we talked at the airport. I know you want me too. Let's just throw caution to the wind and make love right here, right now. Your wife doesn't have to know. It's just one night."

For split second he felt the heat of their bodies, then he realized he couldn't do that. He loved Shaila too much. He took her arms from around his neck and gently pushed her back. "Listen Cheryl, you're a beautiful woman no doubt about it, but I love my wife too much to disrespect her like this. I don't want to hurt you. I really don't, but I can't. I'm sorry."

She looked up at him with her brown eyes and said, "you're a good man. You know that? Your wife is very lucky to have you. Any other man would have probably given into temptation and forgot all about his wife. Well, I won't keep you, Maybe I'll see you around sometime?" She kissed him on the cheek and turned and walked out the door.

"Damn," she said. "This is going to be harder than I thought.

As soon as John got out of the shower, he ordered room service and then dialed Shaila's cell phone.

"Hello."

"God, it's good to hear your voice," he said.

"Hey baby, how was your flight?"

"It was nice and smooth all the way to Boston."

"I miss you so much," she said.

"I miss you, too. How has your day been? Did you get the Wilson account all sewn up?"

"Let's not talk about work, ok."

"Why? Did something happen?"

"No, nothing, I just don't want to discuss anything but us. You know I can't get the last night we spent together out of my mind. I miss your touch. I wish you were back here next to me."

"I know, me too. I'll be home before you know it."

They talked for about another hour before getting off the phone.

After getting off the phone with her husband, her mind wandered back to Marc and their conversation at the restaurant. Her thoughts went back to Cancun and the night they made love on the beach. She shook her head to break her mind away from that particular memory. "Stop this," she said. "Why are you thinking about Marc Wilson?" She couldn't get him out of her mind. He was in her every thought. She knew she loved John, but was she still in love with Marc after all of these years? After all he had hurt her badly back then and she was so madly in love with him at that time. Maybe she never really got over him. She kept her mind heavy with thoughts until she drifted off to sleep.

Chapter 8

"He didn't take the bait, I practically threw myself at him, and he wasn't interested," Cheryl said.

"Damn! I thought he wouldn't be able to resist you. He's not going to make this easy is he?"

Marc said exasperated. "Just keep trying. You have to get him into bed so you can get it on video."

"Baby, you know I would do anything for you, but I don't feel right about this. I mean he really loves her. I don't think he will take the bait. Maybe you should move on and let it go. You're messing with people's lives here."

"Listen, I'm the one who makes the decisions here. You do as I tell you. I will make your life a living hell. I own you. Don't you forget that. Are we clear? You do what you have to do to get him in that bed. Do you understand me? You don't call me back until the deed is done. You have two days before he leaves to come home. You better make it happen or you'll regret it," he said before disconnecting the call.

Cheryl sat there with the phone in her hand and cried. She didn't want to do this, but she didn't have a choice. He would make her life a living hell. After all he did to help her out when she was down and out.

A little over a year ago she was strung out on cocaine and heroin. She had stopped him one day and tried to solicit sex from him. She needed money for another hit. He felt sorry for her so he put her into a rehab clinic, which he paid for out of his own pocket. After her stint in rehab, he cleaned her up and gave her a place to live. His only requirement was that she stay clean. If she fell off the wagon, he would cut her off completely. So far she was doing very well. She had been clean for a little over 6 months now. She wouldn't have anywhere to go if he kicked her out. She couldn't risk him getting mad and retaliating against her.

She took several of her sleeping pills her doctor prescribed to help her sleep and poured them onto the table. She began to crush them with the bottom of her coffee cup until they were the texture of sand. She poured the crushed pills into a little white pouch, sealed it up, and put it into her purse. She picked up her purse, her cell phone, and headed out of her hotel room. She hailed a cab, and once that cab stopped, she gave the driver the hotel where John was staying.

John came back to his hotel room after a long day of speaking on Pediatrics and answering questions. He loved his work, and he loved speaking on the issue, but it was just so tiring. All he wanted to do was take a nice hot shower, call Shaila, and relax for a while. He was about to get into the shower when he heard a knock on the door. He sighed and opened the door. Cheryl stood on the other side of the door.

"I came here to apologize for the other day. I was wrong, and I feel so badly for putting you in that situation. I hope there are no hard feelings," she said with a smile. "I brought some sparkling cider as a peace offering. I didn't want you to think I was trying to get you drunk and seduce you. I just want to talk. Can I come in please?"

"Sure come on in. I'll get some glasses. Have a seat." He walked into the other room and brought out two glasses. She poured the cider into the glasses purposely overflowing them so he would have to get a towel to clean up the mess. John got up to grab a towel to clean up the mess. While he was gone, she took the packet full of sleeping pills and poured it into his glass and swished it around to dissolve the remnants. She put the glass down where he left it. He came back into the room and cleaned up the mess.

"I'm sorry I spilled the drinks. I'm so clumsy."

"That's ok, accidents happen. It can be easily cleaned up."

They made small talk while drinking. After about an hour and half or so, John began to get sleepy. He was to the point he couldn't keep his head up. He finally passed out on the couch. After making sure he was completely passed out, she undressed him, taking much pleasure in staring at his rippled abs. This man was beautiful. She undressed herself completely, standing there for a few minutes feeling guilty and ashamed of what she was about to do.

"I'm so sorry for doing this to you, but I don't have a choice," she whispered to herself. She climbed on top of him placing his hands on her hips and pressing record with her cell phone aimed at them. She started gyrating her hips and moaning like she and John were having sex. She made sure the camera got John in the picture so there was no mistake as to who was in the image. She kissed him on the lips to make it look like they were kissing each other. She let it record for a few minutes and then turned it off. Believing she had enough on video to make it look convincing, she got up and dressed. She put a blanket over his naked body, gave him one last glance, whispered "I'm sorry," and walked out of his hotel room.

John woke up a couple of hours later confused why he was lying nude on the couch when he didn't even remember getting undressed. He turned and looked at the clock on the wall above the entertainment center. The time read seven fifteen p.m. The only thing he remembered was drinking cider with Cheryl and talking. He didn't even remember falling asleep. What the hell happened? He thought to himself. Where the hell did Cheryl go? And where the hell were his clothes? All of these questions were swimming around in his head, but there were no answers. Except that he had seen his clothes draped over the chair sitting opposite the couch. He got up and walked naked into the bathroom and turned on the shower. After about twenty minutes, he came out, dried himself off and put on a pair of shorts and a t-shirt. He called down and ordered a cheeseburger, fries, and a coke. He called Shaila and talked to her for about an hour about their days. He didn't mention the encounter with Cheryl because he didn't know how to explain any of it. He was absolutely sure nothing sexually happened between them even though he couldn't remember. He told Shaila he loved her and he would be home the next day. He said goodbye and hung up the phone.

Cheryl sat down on her couch in her hotel room with her cellphone in her hand. She was feeling so guilty about what she had just done she was in tears. It was tearing away a her. She wondered how she got herself into this mess, and how she was going to get out. One option was to erase the image, but she would have to deal with Marc. She knew Marc would make her regret it for the rest of her life. The only option she had was going through with the plan Marc had set forth. John was a smart man. There was no doubt he would figure out what she had done to him. Then he would more than likely come after her as well. She was dealing with a double edged sword. She knew Marc would be calling soon to get an update. She decided to email Marc the video, but she was not proud of herself in the least. She felt tremendous guilt. She knew she was ruining lives by making the video. The phone rang interrupting her thoughts. She knew instantly who it was. She let it ring three times before she finally answered.

"Hello."

"Is it done?" Marc asked.

"It's done," she said, agitated.

"Good. You really came through for me. I knew you could do it. I'll see you when you get home. Make sure you email the video to me as soon as you get back into town. I'm going to wait until just the right time to email the video to Shaila." She disconnected the phone and cried.

Chapter 9

Shaila was so excited John was coming home. She missed him so much. She hadn't seen him in three days and she was feeling those urges. She had left the office early to get the house ready. She had prepared medium prime rib, baked potato with butter and sour cream, and melted cheddar cheese and bacon bits on top, mixed vegetables and creme brulee for dessert. She also had a bottle of champagne chilling in the bucket. This time she was going to make sure they ate before anything transpired between them. She dimmed the lights and lit candles throughout the dining room. She knew he would be coming in soon because he called her from the car telling her he was about ten minutes away. She was wearing a black spaghetti strap dress that showed off her hourglass figure and black heels. All she needed now was her husband. Everything was set.

Shaila heard the key turn in the lock and saw the door open. There he was, her husband, her reason for living. He looked at her with a smile. He set his luggage by the door, took her into his arms and kissed her passionately.

"I missed you so much," he said with a husky voice.

"I missed you, too. I have dinner waiting for us in the dining room. I made your favorite prime rib. This time we're going to eat before we start anything else." she said with a wink.

"Great, I'm starving. I didn't eat on the plane. I was hoping you cooked."

They ate dinner together in the dining room laughing, talking, and drinking champagne. He was tired from the flight and the busy schedule in Boston, but he wasn't too tired to be with his wife. They finished eating dinner, and he complimented her on the dinner and how she looked. Shaila took the dishes into the kitchen and he began kissing her neck. "Leave them for later," he said. "I want to make love to you right now. I can't wait any longer." He took his hands and placed them underneath her dress. He slid off her black panties and dropped them to the floor. "Don't you want to go to the bedroom?" She asked,

"No, I want you right here, right now."

He lifted her dress up over her head and dropped it to the floor. He looked at her incredible body and caressed her breasts and her lips with his fingers. While he was pleasuring her with his strong hands, she unbuttoned his shirt and slid it off. She unbuttoned his pants, and slid them down to the ground along with his silk boxers. She began to kiss him up his leg and around his genital area. He stood there with his head back and his eyes closed sliding his hands through her hair moaning in ecstasy. He lifted her to her feet, placed her on top of the sink and entered her. He gently thrusted inside her. He was on the brink of unprofound pleasure when she let out a scream. He came shortly after he knew she was satisfied.

"You never cease to amaze me," she said to him.

He gave her a seductive smile and a wink. He picked her up into his arms and carried her upstairs to the bedroom. They made love again and again until they were both worn out. They fell asleep embraced in each other's arms.

It was a beautiful Saturday morning, and after a hectic week, Shaila and John just wanted to spend the weekend in bed. Unfortunately, John was on call for the next week. He wasn't supposed to be on call until the following week, but the Doctor who was supposed to be on call had a death in the family. John was next on the rotation list.

"I'm sorry sweetie. I know you wanted to spend the weekend in Vermont. I will make it up to you. I promise," John said.

"I know, sweetie. It's not your fault. I understand," she said, kissing his hand. "I think I'm going to send flowers to the funeral home. It's the least we can do since we can't attend the funeral," she said.

"That's a good idea. You are so thoughtful and sweet," he gave her a hug. "Would you like me to fix you some breakfast? I can whip something up while you're taking your bath."

"That would be great. Will you be joining me for breakfast?" She asked.

"I think that could be arranged." He gave her a kiss before she stepped into her bath.

Shaila's Saturday morning ritual was to take a long hot bath to wind down and relax after a grueling week of work. Her water was extremely hot. Just the way she liked it. The hotter the better. She put in her lavender beads and bath bubbles. She had ten scented candles surrounding her jacuzzi. The jacuzzi was designed for two people with stairs on both sides to climb down into the water. It had jets all around to give a full body massage. She put her hair up into a bun on top of her head. She used a plush towel to support her head while she relaxed in the tub. She shut her eyes and drifted into heaven.

John was in the kitchen finishing up breakfast. He prepared an omelet with cheese, bacon, hash brown potatoes, and biscuits. He made her favorite hot drink. She liked coffee mixed with cocoa and sugar, He had regular coffee with milk and sugar. He was all set to sit down and have breakfast with Shaila when his cell phone rang. It was the hospital. One of his patient's fever had spiked to 104 degrees and the nurse couldn't bring the fever under control, and they were concerned. He gave the nurse instructions, and told her he would be there as soon as he could. Shaila was still upstairs, and he didn't want to disturb her while she was soaking in the jacuzzi, so he left her a note. He covered up the breakfast and left for the hospital.

Shaila walked downstairs ready to eat breakfast with John to find him not there. A note was sitting on the kitchen table. She read the note, then sat down to eat her breakfast by herself. She finished her breakfast and cleaned up the dishes. She changed into her blue jeans, her Yale college t-shirt and a pair of white socks. She decided to go into her office and do some work. She rarely worked on Saturdays, but since John wasn't there she might as well go over some documents. She came across Marc's contract and thought back to the dinner they had at La Maison. She thought back to their conversation. How they laughed and reminisced about old college times. That brought a smile to her face.

After working for a couple of hours, Shaila decided she would call her mother, and see how she was doing. She talked to her mother at least once a week. Sometimes more when she had time. They talked about what was going on with their lives, and trips they had taken in the past few months. They talked for about an hour catching up. They said their I love yous and hung up the phone.

It was about three o'clock in the afternoon. Shaila sat in the den reading a book when the phone rang.

"Hello," she answered.

"Hi baby," John said. I'm still at the hospital. I'm probably going to be here for a while. Things are crazy here. I called to check in on you to see what you were up to." he explained. "I'm sorry I skipped out on you without saying goodbye."

"It's ok. I went over some documents, talked to my mother, and now I'm reading a book. Is everything going ok with your patient?"

"Yes, everything turned out fine. We got her fever under control. I ordered the nurses to monitor her every hour. Look, baby I have to go. I'm being paged. I love you." before she could say anything back, he hung up.

"It had been three hours since she and John talked. He hadn't called back, or come home, so she decided to go to a cafe down the block to get something to eat. She ordered a chicken sandwich, fries, and diet coke. Waiting for her order, someone tapped her on the shoulder. She turned and there was Marc standing behind her. He was wearing blue jeans, a red short sleeved buttoned down shirt and Nike tennis shoes. "He looked so good standing there," she said to herself.

"Well, hey there stranger. What are you doing here?" He asked.

"I'm getting me a sandwich to take back to the house to eat."

"Where's John? Is he out of town for another conference?"

"No, he's at the hospital. He's on call this week. What are you doing over here? I thought you were out of town on business."

"I was. I finished up early and flew back today. That's the perk of owning your own private jet. I didn't want to stay in LA, so I decided to come home. I got hungry and came down here to get something to eat. You know I'm not much of a cook. Carmen, the lady that cleans and cooks for me, has the weekend off. I was supposed to be out of town otherwise she would have cooked for me." Little did she know, he really came there hoping to run into her. Luck had it, he did.

"Miss, here's your order."

"Thanks, she said with a smile. "I have to get back in case John calls. I don't have my cell phone with me. I'll see you later."

"Yeah, I'll see you later."

She walked in the direction of her penthouse. She glanced back to catch him staring at her. She smiled and waved. She turned back around and continued walking toward her penthouse.

"Just a matter of time," he whispered to himself. He walked in the opposite direction to his Maserati, got in and drove off.

Chapter 10

"What are you going to do with the video?" Cheryl asked. "Are you going to send it to Shaila?"

"I haven't decided how to play it yet. I have to find and angle. I have to get her to trust me again."

"What is your obsession with this Shaila woman? She is your drug like heroin and cocaine used to be mine. Weren't you the one who told me being hooked on something was bad for your health?"

"Your situation is totally different than mine. I won't end up dead with my obsession. On the other hand, if you go back to your old ways of shooting up and selling yourself, you will end up dead on a street corner somewhere. Oh and by the way, I hope I made myself clear about that. I won't hesitate to kick your ass to the curb if you slip up just once, believe that."

"I got it! I got it! I'm clean. I haven't touched the stuff in over six months and don't intend to. Speaking of someone getting killed, you don't think John will come after you if and when he finds out you set him up with the video. He's a smart man. He will figure it out. Ok, just indulge me for a second, and let me say that I don't feel right about this, but I will keep my mouth shut."

"You'd better for your sake," he threatened.

"Do you think I'm about to throw away my meal ticket? I may be a recovering junkie, but I'm not stupid. Well, at least not anymore," she sassed back.

He gave a soft chuckle. "If we play our cards right and be patient, everything will fall into place."

"I thought you said you loved Shaila and you would never do anything to hurt her?"

"I do love her."

"Oh you do, do yo? Have you really thought this through? Do you think this whole scheme you have concocted is going to have her jumping for joy? She asked sarcastically. "By the way, you still haven't told me what you are planning to do."

"I'm going to gain her trust. Reignite the feelings we used to share. She has to be confused as to what she wants. Does she want me? Does she want John? What am I feeling?" Giving her scenarios of what he was explaining to her. "When I think she is confused enough for my satisfaction, I'll email her the video anonymously. She will view the video, devastated that her perfect husband cheated on her and come running back to me. Of course, I will be very sympathetic and consoling. One thing will lead to another, and I will have Shaila back right where she belongs," he said with a devilish grin.

"Oh, that's balanced," she said sarcastically. "Now I know how you became so successful, your mind is twisted. You don't give a damn about anyone but yourself, including Shaila. You will do anything and use anyone to get what you want. You claim to love Shaila so much, yet you are planning on tearing her whole world apart, and for what to get back what you screwed up in the first place."

Before she could say another word, he grabbed her by the throat and threw her up against the wall. "You seem to forget all I have done for you. You think about that before you pass judgment on me," he said furiously.

The devil had just taken over. The Look in his eyes chilled her to the bone. She shook violently. She couldn't breathe. She was gasping for air. He finally let her go and stepped back. She didn't move. It was like her feet were frozen to the floor. Her mind was screaming run, but her butt was screaming you better stay right where you are because if you move, he will do something worse. He gave her a stern look then he turned and walked away.

Shaila woke up the next morning with John lying next to her. She had gone to bed around twelve thirty and John still wasn't home. She didn't know when he had gotten home. She was going to wake him for church, but she decided not to. He was probably tired from working all night. She decided to go to church without him.

She and John usually went to brunch after church, but Shaila decided to skip brunch and go home. She was sure John would be up by then, and she didn't want him to worry where she was even though he probably knew she was at church. She said goodbye to everyone outside of the church after the service, and walked back to her SUV. She drove the five miles back to the penthouse hoping John would be up and waiting for her. She parked her SUV in the parking garage next to her building and proceeded up to her penthouse.

Thinking John would be there waiting for her, she ran into the penthouse. Afterall, she hadn't seen John very much since Friday. She looked forward to spending some time with him. She walked into the penthouse, but she didn't hear anything. John was nowhere to be found. She found a note on the dining room table. *Baby, I got called into the hospital again. I'll call you later. I love you. J*

She didn't have anything else to do so she called Jasmine. Jasmine was Greg's wife. She knew Greg was out of time on business and the kids were probably at her mother's house for the day. She invited Jasmine to brunch. They decided to meet at a nice little eatery not too far from Jasmine's house. Jasmine was the first to arrive. She was an attractive woman. She had short black hair, dark brown eyes, and a bronze skin tone. She was about two inches shorter than Shaila. Shaila got there and Jasmine stood up to give her a hug. As soon as they sat down, the waiter came over to take their drink orders.

"What's up girl? I haven't seen you in a while. How's everything?" Jasmine asked.

"Everything's going well. Work is wonderful. We just landed a multi-billion dollar account. Things are going very well. I can't complain. What about you? How are my beautiful nieces and nephews? I'm going to need my fix soon. I miss them so much. I miss all of you. It's a shame we don't get together more often. I mean we don't live far from each other at all."

The waiter came back and took their lunch orders.

"I know what you mean. I know Greg misses his baby sis. So do the kids. I think it's mostly the spoiling they miss. They always know when they see Auntie Sha they will get something," Jasmine said laughing.

"Are they with their grandmother today?"

"You know it. They always go to her house on Sundays to give Greg and me some free time."

"When will Greg be back from his business trip?"

"Tomorrow. I really miss him. He's been gone for a week, but he calls at least twice a day. Speaking of which, where is John today?"

"He's on call this week. He's been at the hospital all weekend. I haven't seen him much at all. I'm surprised he hasn't called me. He must be really busy."

"Is he always this busy when he's on call?"

"No, not always. He sometimes doesn't have to go anywhere, he can tell the nurses what to do over the phone. However, he's covering for two other doctors, so he's probably swamped."

"Hello ladies."

Shaila turned around to see Marc standing behind her.

"Marc, what a pleasant surprise. What are you doing here?" Shaila asked.

"I was having lunch with some friends and I saw you sitting over here. I hope you don't mind me coming over to say hi."

"No, not at all. Jasmine, this is Marc Wilson. Marc, this is my sister-in-law Jasmine," Shaila introduced.

Marc shook Jasmine's hand and said, "it's a pleasure to meet you. Are you married to Greg or Tommy?" He asked.

"Greg, do you know him?"

"Yeah, I should. I dated Shaila for three years while we were in college. I met him quite a few times. Tommy, Greg, Shaila, and I along with their girlfriends at that time, went to Cancun together one spring break," he looked at Shaila with a familiar smirk. I'm surprised Shaila never mentioned it."

"It never came up," Shaila said.

"Well, I better get back to my party. I just came over to say hi. I don't want to be rude to my friends, but truth be told, I would much rather be here having lunch with you two lovely ladies. Jasmine, it was a pleasure meeting you. Shaila, I'll see you soon," he turned and walked to his table.

Shaila couldn't help but look at his butt as he walked away. She gradually tried to play it off by pretending there was a cramp in her neck.

"Girl don't even try to front. I saw you checking out his butt. Don't feel bad I was checking it out right along with you. Damn. Shaila, he is fine. Not to dog John in the least, because he is a fine specimen also, but why in the hell did you let that hunk of man get away? Whoa girl if I wasn't married, you would have to pry me off him with a crowbar. And what is that I hear? Shaila, I'll see you soon, Are you creepin?" Jasmine asked with a smile.

"Would you stop? No, we are not creepin. He's a new client to my firm. What he means is we will see each other at the office from time to time."

"So he's the big client you were talking about when you first came in. Um hum."

"Girl, you're putting too much into this. He and I are just friends. We haven't seen each other in years."

"What does John say about all of this? Isn't he the least bit concerned that his wife has a client who's an ex boyfriend?"

"He doesn't know Marc and I dated. I never told him about Marc. He just thinks he's a client that's contracted with the firm. Besides, he has no reason to suspect anything is going on."

"Uh huh, then why not tell him?" Jasmine said, picking up her fork to eat her salad.

"Tell him what? Oh come on. There's nothing to tell. Nothing is going on between us. We're just friends. How many times do I have to tell you that?" Shaila said, trying to convince herself.

"Did I say there was anything going on? Who are you trying to convince here, me or yourself?" Jasmine asked, giving her an inquisitive look.

Shaila let out a sigh and began to eat her chicken salad.

"Would you ladies care for anything else?" The waiter asked.

"No, not for me, thank you," Shaila said.

"No, thank you," Jasmine said back.

"Well, you ladies have a pleasant afternoon and please come back and see us again soon."

"Sir, you forgot to give us the check," Shaila said with a confused look on her face.

"Your check has already been paid."

"Paid. May I ask by whom?" Shaila asked, surprised.

"That gentleman sitting over there." He pointed to Marc. As Shaila looked in Marc's direction, he looked at her, lifted his glass, and smiled. She smiled back and mouthed, "Thank you."

He nodded back as if to say your welcome.

"From where I'm sitting it looks like he may want to be a little more than just friends," Jasmine said.

Shaila let out a sigh and continued eating her salad.

Shaila came into her penthouse and threw her purse onto the couch. She headed to the bedroom to change her clothes. She put on a pair of black leggings and a t-shirt. She went downstairs to the den and checked the messages to see if John called. There was one message.

"Hi sweetie, I guess you're not home. I'm just calling to see how you were. I miss you. I hope to be home soon. I'm going to try to get home at a decent hour today. I'm sorry I missed you. I love you."

She sat down on the couch, laid her head back, and put her feet up on the coffee table. She picked up the remote to the television and turned it on. She started flipping through the channels to see if anything good was on. Nothing looked good to her so she turned off the television and went to look for a book to read. She just wasn't in the mood to read or watch television. She thought maybe she would do some shopping. She hadn't been shopping in a while, but she really didn't want to do that either. What she really wanted to do was spend time with John but that wasn't an option. Her mind drifted back to that night she and Marc spent in Cancun. The night they made love on the beach. They couldn't sleep that night so they decided they would take a walk on the beach. The water was crystal blue. So clear they could see the bottom. The tides rolled in from the ocean. The smell of the salt air engulfed them. They walked along the beach holding hands and talking. Suddenly Marc turned Shaila towards him and looked deep into her eyes, bent his head to meet hers, and then kissed her with such passion it was as if a thunderbolt went off in her head. With their tongues intertwining with each other, they both groaned with each stroke. Shaila took her hands and started to caress his back up and down with the tips of her fingernails. He slowly kissed her neck and worked his way downward to the center part of her breasts. He slowly reached around the back of her bathing suit top and unfastened it. He let it drop to the sand and proceeded to suck on her nipples. He gently pushed her down to the sand and positioned himself on top of her. As he kissed her all over, the tide came underneath them making it even more exciting. He took her bikini bottoms off. She was completely nude, and the only thing he had on were his shorts.

"We can't do this out here," Shaila said.

"Why not? No one is watching us, but if you want me to stop, I will. Just let me know. I don't want to do anything you don't feel comfortable doing."

"I want you so bad right now, but what if someone walks by and sees us?"

He continued to kiss her all over. It really wasn't supposed to go that far. Just a little kissing and foreplay, but he couldn't help himself. He couldn't wait any longer. He had this beautiful naked woman lying underneath him. His erection was as hard as steel. He started to raise himself off her, when she said, "no, I want you to make love to me right here."

"Are you sure?" He asked.

"I'm sure."

She pulled him down on top of her and pulled his shorts over his perfectly round butt and threw them to the sand next to her bathing suit. He slowly entered her temple with gentle thrusts at first and he sped up a little more with each thrust. She rocked her hips in sync with his. He pleasured her so well she was ready to explode, but she held it back. It felt too good to her. After a few thrusts, she couldn't hold on any longer. She exploded into complete ecstasy. Marc exploded soon after her. He kissed her and said, "I love you, Shaila."

"I love you, too, Marc."

"Shaila, hello, Shaila." someone calling her name interrupted her thoughts. It was John.

"Shaila, where were you? I've been calling your name for the past few minutes. You must have been in deep thought you didn't even hear me. What were you thinking about?" John asked.

"I was thinking about you," she lied. "I missed you. I didn't hear you come in. I'm sorry." She got up and gave him a big hug and a kiss.

"Are you here to stay?" She asked.

"I'm afraid not, baby. I have to go back to the hospital. I have to assist Dr. Martin in surgery. I just came home to pick up a few things I needed to take back with me and to see you for a few minutes.

"When are you going to be back?"

"I'm not sure, sweetie. This surgery could take up to twelve hours. I will call you as soon as I can. I have to get back to the hospital." He leaned down and kissed her. "I love you."

"I love you, too."

Shaila got out of her SUV and walked into Saks Fifth Avenue to do some shopping. She really wasn't in the mood for shopping, but she didn't want to sit at home by herself another day. She would have called one of her friends, but they were all spending time with their families. Jasmine was going to her mother's to pick up her kids, so

HER DANGEROUS LOVER

that was out. She could have gone over to see them, but she decided against it. Jasmine probably wasn't even home yet. She looked at some blouses that she was interested in buying. She picked the one she liked and flung it over her arm. She might as well buy shoes and accessories to go with it. She ended up picking up shoes, earrings, a belt, a skirt, and a pair of pants to match the blouse. She took her items up to the sales lady and checked out. The sales lady gave her a big smile and a thank you for shopping at Saks and told her to please come back soon. She was happy because she knew she would get a sizable commission off that sale. Shaila walked down the mall to other stores when she heard someone call her name.

"Shaila." She turned around and Sara walked up beside her.

"Sara, how are you?"

"I'm doing well. I see you went on a shopping spree," she said, looking down at the bags Shaila was carrying.

"Yeah, well I was bored sitting at home so I came shopping."

"Where's John?"

That was the question on everyone's mind lately. Where's John?

"He's on call this week. He's assisting in a surgery."

"I guess that means you didn't make it to Vermont this weekend?"

"No, we didn't. Maybe next weekend."

"Are you here by yourself?" Shaila asked.

"No, I'm here with some friends. They are looking around in Bloomingdales. I saw you so I decided to come and say hi. I better get back. I'll see you tomorrow."

"See you tomorrow."

Shaila was sick of shopping. After all, she really didn't want to come in the first place. She decided to go home and see what was on her movie channels and watch some movies. Maybe a movie with Samuel L Jackson. He was one of her favorite actors. She got home and put her shopping bags in the bedroom. She threw some popcorn into the microwave, popped a movie into the DVD and sat up for a night of watching Sam.

Chapter 11

Shaila sat in her office looking over some paperwork on her desk. She had a big deposition she had to prepare. Her mind was wandering all over the place. She just couldn't concentrate. She hadn't seen John practically at all over the weekend. She was already in bed by the time he came home last night. In fact, she didn't even know he was there until she woke up this morning and saw him lying next to her. She wanted to wake him up, but she didn't. He needed his rest. She would ask him tonight how the surgery went. She got up from her desk and walked over to her window and stared out into nowhere. She had so much going through her mind. She was having a hard time concentrating. Her thoughts were of Marc much to her dismay. She couldn't be thinking about Marc all the time. She was a married woman. She should be thinking about her husband. She let out a sigh and tilted her back. She needed to spend more time with her husband. If she could just spend more time with him, she wouldn't be thinking about Marc all the time. Her private phone line rang. She deduced it was probably John calling because he was the only one who really called her on that line.

"This is Shaila."

"Hey sweetie, how are you?"

"Hey baby, I was hoping you would call. I missed you last night. I didn't hear you come in. Why didn't you wake me?"

"I'm sorry. I didn't want to wake you. I didn't get in until after 2 a.m. Besides, I was so beat, all I wanted to do was go to sleep."

"Are you at home right now?"

"No, I'm at the office. I wanted to let you know I will probably be late coming home tonight. We have a hospital staff meeting tonight. Don't wait up for me.

"John, I realize you're busy, but I haven't seen you much at all this weekend. When are we going to spend some time together? I'm tired of eating and going to bed alone. I know I sound selfish right now, but I miss you."

"I miss you, too, sweetie, and I'm sorry. I promise I will make it up to you. After this week, I will have more free time to spend with you."

"I know," she began.

"Sweetie, I have to go now. I have a patient waiting for me. I love you." He hung up leaving Shaila holding the phone. Shaila put the phone back on the receiver and turned her chair back around to the window and leaned her head back looking up at the ceiling.

Shaila was going to try and stay up and wait for John to come home. Even though she had a really hectic day and she was extremely tired, she wanted to talk to John. She hadn't talked to him about anything since he came back from Boston. She wanted to know what happened on this trip. It was late, about twelve o'clock. Shaila was still up reading a book in bed when she heard the front door open. She heard footsteps walking around downstairs. She walked into the kitchen and saw him standing in front of the open refrigerator door pouring himself a glass of milk.

"Hey sweetie, I thought you would be asleep by now. I told you I would be late and not to wait up."

"I know. I couldn't sleep. I wanted to wait up for you. I was hoping you would get home early enough so we could talk."

"We were done with the staff meeting early, and I was on my way home when I got paged by the hospital. I had to go back."

"Are you tired? Do you want me to give you a massage to help you relax?"

"No, not tonight, baby. I just want to go upstairs, take my clothes off, wash up, and go to sleep."

He walked upstairs to the bedroom with Shaila following behind him. She went and lied on the bed with nothing on but a t-shirt and a pair of panties. John took off his clothes and put them on the chair so he would remember to take them to the dry cleaners the next day. All he had on were his white silk boxer shorts. Shaila couldn't help but look at his rippled muscles. He really turned her on. He walked into the bathroom and washed up and brushed his teeth. He came out and got into the bed next to her. She planned to leave him alone and let him sleep until she saw his beautiful body. She couldn't control herself. She leaned over to him and started kissing him. First she kissed his lips, and then she headed downward to his neck. She was kissing him down his neck when he suddenly stopped her.

"Not tonight ok, sweetie, I'm too tired," he said, kissing her on the forehead. He turned over to his side with his back to her and fell asleep. She gave out a long drawn out sigh and turned onto her side and laid there feeling rejected. She finally fell asleep, but her thoughts were not of John. They were of Marc.

"What's up with you John? Are you and Shaila fighting?" Jerry asked.

"No, why do you ask?"

"Well, one reason is you have been spending a lot of time at the hospital lately."

"I am on call this week, remember? I get paged and I have to respond. You know how it goes." he said sarcastically.

"Don't give me that crap. I've read the chart notes on the patient's you were called about, and you could have given instructions over the phone. And another thing, you know good and well you didn't have to come to the hospital to assist Dr. Martin in surgery. He has done that particular surgery a hundred times. So I will ask you again. What's going on? Why are you avoiding Shaila? Talk to me, what's going on?"

"I'm not avoiding her. I just don't know what to tell her when she asks about my trip to Boston. I know she will want all the details, and I don't know what to tell her."

"Don't know how to tell her what exactly? Did you cheat on Shaila?"

"No, I mean I don't think so. Honestly, I don't know."

"What do you mean you don't know? You either did or you didn't. It's a simple question."

John told Jerry everything that happened in Boston. Everything from the moment he met Cheryl, to what happened in his hotel room. He went into detail about how she followed him to his hotel. How she came to his room and tried to seduce him. He told him what had happened the night he woke up lying on the couch naked. Jerry looked at him with a puzzled look on his face.

"Ok man, let me ask you this. Do you think you had sex with this woman?"

"No, I don't think I did, but I don't know. I don't remember anything."

"What exactly do you remember about that night?"

"I remember Cheryl coming to the door apologizing for the night before, drinking cider and talking. The next thing I knew I was on the couch naked with a blanket covered over me."

"Did you leave her alone at any time when she came with the drink? I mean you said you invited her in and went to get glasses for the drinks, right?"

"Right."

"Did you leave her alone at any time after you got the glasses and poured the drinks?"

"Yes the drinks overflowed onto the table, and I went into the bathroom to get a towel to clean it up."

"If I didn't know any better, I would say she drugged you. She put something into your drink when you left the room."

"But why? What would she have to gain? I don't even know her. I mean I was honest with her from the start. I told her I was in love with Shaila, and I couldn't be unfaithful to her. I don't know what's going on here. How can I explain any of this to Shaila and make her understand when I don't even understand it myself? What have I gotten myself into, Jerry?"

"I don't know, but if I were you, I would try and find this Cheryl woman to give you some answers. You didn't get a last name did you?"

"No, I didn't even think to ask her."

"Maybe you should go home and tell Shaila the truth about what happened. Tell her what you do know exactly. This Cheryl person could be setting you up."

"Setting me up for what?"

"You're a very wealthy man, not to mention your parents. If she knows who you are and who your family is, which she probably does, this could be a blackmail attempt to get money out of you."

John rubbed his temples and let out a sigh.

Shaila sat in her office thinking about what happened the night before. He was too tired to make love to her. He had never been too tired to make love to her. Why was last night different? Deep in thought she was interrupted by a knock on her door.

"Hey Shaila, what's up?" Sara asked.

"Nothing, just going over some contract."

"Anything I can help you with?"

"No, thank you, I can handle it. This stuff is pretty basic. Is there something you need?"

"I was on my way out to get some lunch. I thought maybe you would like to join me."

"No, thank you. I'm not hungry, rain check?"

"Ok, sure." Sara turned to walk away, but stopped and turned to face Shaila again. "Shaila, what's wrong? You don't seem like yourself lately."

Shaila looked up from her desk, threw her pen on top of the papers she was working on and let out a deep breath. "John has been on call this week, and I haven't seen him much lately. I guess I'm a little lonely. I miss him. I know I'm being selfish. It's his job, but I want some of his time too. I'm sorry. I'm just going on and on aren't I? This is not your problem.

"You don't have to apologize to me, Shaila. You're always here to listen to me when I have a problem. Let me return the favor. Come on, talk to me."

"I didn't see him for three days when he was in Boston, but I did talk to him every night. He comes back, and we spend Friday night together, and now he's on call all week. I've spent a total of maybe twenty minutes with him the entire weekend. He came home around midnight last night and he's too tired to talk to me. I guess I'm just putting too much into it. I know he loves me and he would spend time with me if he weren't on call. I knew what I was getting into when I married a surgeon. I knew being a surgeon's wife wouldn't be easy, but something has changed with John. I can sense it. Some of the things he's doing lately, he has never done in the past. He has never stayed all day and all night at the hospital, let alone the weekend. He would always come home and spend a couple of hours with me and then go back to the hospital. When I tried talking to him this past weekend, he wouldn't talk to me. He said he was too tired and he wanted to go to sleep. He always talks to me even when he's dead tired. Something's not right." She let out a sigh. "If I didn't know any better, I would think there was another woman."

"No, I don't believe that. He wouldn't cheat on you. He loves you too much to do that. There has to be another explanation. Maybe he was just tired like he said. Give him the benefit of the doubt, but make him talk to you tonight regardless if he's tired or not. Don't jump to any conclusions until you talk to him first, ok? I'm sure it's nothing. Keep your chin up. Everything will be ok."

"Thanks Sara, I will."

"Listen, I'm going to get some lunch. Are you sure you don't want to come?"

"Yeah, I'm sure."

"Ok, call me if you need to talk some more."

"I will. Thanks for letting me vent."

"It's ok. I'll see you later."

Sara turned and began walking down the hall when she noticed Marc standing not far from Shaila's office.

"Hello Mr. Wilson, can I help you?"

"Um, no, um…I was looking for Ben's office," he said nervously.

She pointed to a door down at the end of the hall.

"Thank you."

"My pleasure."

Marc turned and walked down the hall leaving Sara with a skeptical look on her face. He was listening to our conversation. She thought. She walked back to Shaila's Office. "Shaila, have you spoken to Marc lately?"

"Well, we had dinner one night when John was in Boston and talked about old times. Why do you ask?"

"No reason, I was just curious."

So Shaila is feeling lonely. Hubby isn't taking care of business. She thinks there might be another woman. He thought to himself, Marc smiled a devilish grin. This was the perfect time to email the video. He reached inside his jacket pocket and pulled out his cell phone. "Download the images on DVD and sent it to Shaila," he said to the person on the other line.

Chapter 12

Shaila came home from work to find a package addressed to her sitting in front of her door. She brought the package inside and put it on the couch along with the rest of the mail. She went upstairs and put on a pair of sweats and a t-shirt. She came downstairs and started going through the mail. Nothing interesting, just bills and junkmail. She put them to the side, picked up the package, and opened it up. She found a DVD. Puzzled, she put the DVD into the player and pressed play. She was shocked to see her husband having sex with another woman on DVD. She quickly turned it off, put her hands over her face and cried. She didn't know what to do. She was in complete shock. She had loved that man for ten years. She had been there for him through thick and thin. She had been his lover and his friend. How could he do this to her? She had all these thoughts running through her head when she heard John come through the front door. She was sitting in the dark when John came into the den looking for her.

"Shaila, are you home?" He walked into the den and saw her sitting on the couch in the dark. He turned the light on. "Why are you sitting in the dark?" He walked over to her and noticed she was crying. "Baby, what's wrong? Is somebody hurt? What is it?" He asked worriedly.

"No, no one is hurt." With the remote in her hand, she pressed play. John was in total shock when he saw himself on video with Cheryl naked on top of him having sex.

"Baby, I…" He tried to explain, but she put her hands up in front of his face as if to say I don't want to hear it. She got up from the couch and walked past him to the bedroom and shut the door. He followed her up to the bedroom. "Baby, please let me explain," he pleaded with her.

"Explain what? I think it's pretty self explanatory, don't you?" She cried uncontrollably. "I'm so stupid I can't believe I didn't see this. I don't understand. Why would you do this to me? How could you humiliate me like this? Who is she? Was this in Boston? Did you sleep with this woman while you were in Boston?"

"Yes, no, I mean I don't know."

"What do you mean you don't know? You're butt naked with a strange woman on DVD having sex with her. How are you going to stand there and say you don't know? Let the record show, you are on DVD having sex with a woman who's not your wife. It doesn't get more clear than that. A video is worth a thousand words and that video says it all. Face the facts John, you're caught," she yelled.

"Shaila, I know this looks bad, but I can explain. I met this girl at the airport before I left for Boston," he began.

She cut him off before he could say anything else. "You mean to tell me, you slept with a woman you met in an airport?"

"No, Shaila, it's not that simple."

"It is that simple! You have such little regard for your wife you invite a strange woman you don't even know up to your room. One thing leads to another, you get carried away in the moment, and you two end up in the bed? Does that about sum it up? Please let me know if I left anything out. Did you think I wouldn't find out? I know you, John. I've noticed changes in you since you came back from Boston. Now I know why. You cheated on me. You bastard, I love you so much. I gave you everything I had, and you threw it away on a one night stand, or have there been more than one?"

"No, Shaila, it wasn't like that at all. Please just let me explain," he pleaded.

"I don't want to hear your lame excuses. I just want you out of here."

"Shaila, you don't mean that."

"The hell I don't. Get out!" She went over and sat on the bed and put her hands over her face and cried. She was so hurt and angry. She couldn't even think straight. John came over and knelt down in front of her. He tried to take her hand, but she jerked it away, got up, and said, "don't touch me, you lying, cheating son of a bitch!. I want you out of this house now! You pack up whatever you need for tomorrow and get out. You can come back for the rest of your stuff tomorrow while I'm at work. I don't want to see you."

"Shaila." Before he could say another word, she turned away from him and stormed out of the bedroom slamming the door behind her. John began packing his suitcase. He went into the bathroom and got his toiletry items and placed them in his bag. He looked at himself in the mirror and tears welled in his eyes. He cried so uncontrollably his vision was blurred. He pulled himself together, zipped his suitcase, and headed out of the bedroom door. He headed down the stairs and went into the den where Shaila sat on the couch. "I'm leaving," he said, trying to get her attention, but she didn't say a word to him. She just stared straight ahead like she didn't hear him. He was hoping she would ask him to stay, but he knew it wasn't going to happen. She was way too angry and hurt to listen to him. "I love you, Shaila." He turned and walked out the front door. As soon as the door shut, Shaila broke down and cried with all the hurt, the anger, and the betrayal she had inside her.

John sat in his office wondering what he was going to do next. He couldn't lose this woman he had loved for all these years. He had to find out what happened in that hotel room. He knew in his heart he didn't sleep with that woman. He just had to prove it. He needed to find Cheryl, but how? He didn't know her last name. All he knew was that she was in real estate if that was the truth. Jerry walked into his office startling him out of his thoughts.

"I take it it didn't go well when you told Shaila what happened in Boston,"

"I didn't have to tell her. Someone had sent her a DVD of Cheryl and me having sex. She kicked me out last night. I've lost her, Jerry," he said with tears in his eyes.

"I'm sorry, John. Where are you staying?"

"The Carlton."

"Cheryl planned this from the beginning, but I don't understand why. Why would she go through all of that just to send the DVD to her? If it was money she was after, she would have come to you first and tried to blackmail you and if you didn't pay her, then she would have sent it to Shaila. But she didn't do that, she just sent the DVD. That doesn't make sense, Something else is going on here, and it has nothing to do with money. Somebody wanted Shaila to think you were cheating on her. You've been set up, my friend."

"I know, but why? Why would Cheryl want to break up my marriage? I have to figure this all out so I can save my marriage and get my wife back. I can't lose her, Jerry. She's my heart, and my reason for being."

"I know. I will help you in any way I can. What can I do?"

"I don't want to get you involved. If this DVD goes public, there goes my career and yours along with it just for being associated with me. I can't put you at risk like that. I'm not too worried about my career right now. All I'm worried about is getting Shaila back. That is my main concern. My career is a distant second."

"I know it is. Whatever happens I will stand by you. I'm not going to let you or your career go down the drain. I will do whatever I can to make sure that doesn't happen and so will your colleagues. If this DVD does get out, no one will turn their back on you. You are too well respected. If it's any consolation, I know you didn't cheat on Shaila."

"Thanks, that means a lot."

"We'll figure this out. I promise."

"So did you talk to John last night?" Sara asked.

Shaila sat at her desk when Sara walked in, She stood looking out her window with her back to the door. Sara couldn't see Shaila had been crying when she first walked in the door. Shaila turned to look at her.

"Shaila, what happened? Are you ok? Why are you crying?"

"John cheated on me when he went to Boston. Someone sent me a DVD of him and some woman having sex." She threw her hands up over her face and began crying uncontrollably. Sara shut the door to give them privacy, and walked over to her and gave her a consoling hug.

"Shaila, I'm so sorry. I don't know what to say. John is the last person I would have thought would cheat. I guess you were right. What did he say?"

"There was nothing he could say. The evidence was all on DVD. He can't charm his way out of this mess. What am I going to do? I love him so much, but I can't be with a man I can't trust. Sara, tell me what am I going to do now?" Shaila sat down in her chair and cried all over again. This time it was continuous tears flowing down her cheeks.

"Why don't you go home and get some rest. You don't need to be here. You're not going to get any work done anyway. Go home. I'll cover anything that comes up."

"I have to work on this deposition. I have to get it done by tomorrow."

"I'm caught up with my work, and I know what needs to be done. I will finish it for you. Don't worry. Now go home. I will call if I need you."

"You will keep this between us? I don't want everyone in the office knowing what happened."

"Of course, I will, No one will find out from me. I promise," she said, giving Shaila another hug. "Call me if you need anything."

Shaila left the building, but she didn't go home. She walked over to Central Park and sat down on a bench. She stared at the people walking, and children playing when Marc came over and sat down next to her.

"Hey beautiful, what are you doing over here?

She turned to him with her eyes red, swollen, and puffy from crying all night into the day.

"Are you ok? Why are you crying?" He put his hands on her face and wiped away her tears. He knew why she was crying and at that particular moment, he felt guilty. He couldn't stand seeing her hurting so much. He truly did love her. It broke his heart to see her crying. It reminded him of the day back in college when she caught Brooke and him in the bed together. The same hurt in her eyes back then was displayed in her eyes this time. She closed her eyes and put her head on his shoulder. She was completely lost and heartbroken.

"Tell me baby, what happened?"

"Someone sent me a DVD of John and some woman having sex while he was in Boston. My husband cheated on me with some strange woman he met in the New York airport. I feel so stupid and humiliated. Why does this keep happening to me? Why do guys I fall in love with cheat on me? What am I doing wrong? First you, now John."

"Baby, I'm so sorry. There's nothing wrong with you. I was the stupid one. I made the mistake. If I could take it back, I would. That stupid mistake cost me everything. It cost me you. As far as John is concerned, I can't speak for him. He must not have been thinking straight. He must have gotten carried away at that moment. I don't know what to tell you. I wish I could take all your hurt away." He truly meant what he said to her. He did what he did to get her back, but he didn't consider the fact she would hurt so badly over it. He didn't expect to feel regret for what he did. "What are you going to do now?"

"I don't know. I'm stuck in a dark tunnel and I can't seem to find a light at the end. My world has been turned upside down." Her eyes welled up with tears. She tried to hold them back, but she couldn't control them.

Marc's heart truly ached for her. "It's ok, baby, get it all out." He was responsible for your hurt. He never considered the consequences of his actions. All he wanted ws Shaila. He wanted the love of his life back.

She pulled away from him and said, "Marc, I'm sorry. I shouldn't be burdening you with my problems. This is my problem and I will deal with it."

"Baby, you don't have to apologize to me. We are still friends aren't we? Friends talk to each other. If you have a problem, please come and talk to me about it. I still care very deeply for you. I never stopped."

"Thank you, Marc, I don't want to come across rude, but I need some time on my own. I need to think about what to do next. Thank you for giving me a shoulder to cry on."

"Anytime."

Shaila got up and walked away. Marc sat on the bench tormented by seeing the woman he loved crying on his shoulder over something he orchestrated. He had to think about the big picture. She was hurting right now, but soon she would be with him and everything would be the way it should be. She would be with him.

Sara was up in Shaila's office looking out the window where Shaila and Marc were talking. She watched as Marc sauntered over and sat down next to Shaila. She watched them nonstop until Shaila got up and walked away. She saw everything that transpired between them. "What is that man up to? There's something about that man I don't trust," she said out loud, but to herself.

"Who are you talking to?" John asked, standing in the doorway of Shaila's office.

"John, how long have you been standing there?"

"I just walked in. I was looking for Shaila. Is she here?"

"No, she left about twenty minutes ago. She wasn't getting any work done. I sent her home. All she could do was stand here and cry. How could you do that to her, John? You of all people, cheating on your wife. I never would have thought in a million years you would do that."

John put his head down in shame. He couldn't say anything to defend himself because he knew she was right. He came into the office and sat down on the couch. Sara came down and sat down next to him.

"Did she tell you everything?"

"Yes, she did."

He put his hand over his face and bent his head down and shook it in shame.

"Tell me you didn't do this. This was all a mistake right?"

Tears welled up in his eyes. "At first I was adamant. I told her I loved Shaila and I wouldn't betray her by cheating on her. But then she came back the next night…"

Sara cut him off before he could say anything else. "Wait, wait a minute. Who is she?

"Cheryl."

"She's the woman on the DVD?"

"Yes."

"She tried to seduce you the night before and you said no?"

"Yes, I told her no."

"Then why the hell would you not say no the second time. That doesn't make sense, John. On the spur of the moment you suddenly decided it was ok to betray your wife. Is that it?" She was infuriated.

"No! And why am I sitting here explaining this to you? You're not the one I need to be convincing. In all honesty, I really don't care what you or anyone else thinks about me! All I care about is what Shaila thinks and getting her back. So if you'll excuse me." He got up and started to walk out the door.

"John, wait. I'm sorry. I shouldn't have gotten into your business like that. I just can't stand to see Shaila hurting so much. I also think of you as a good friend and an upstanding doctor. I thought you and Shaila had the perfect marriage."

"I know. I can't stand to see Shaila hurt either. It breaks my heart knowing I'm at fault one way or another. I just wish I could remember what happened that night."

"You mean you don't remember? Were you drunk?"

"No, we didn't drink alcohol. She brought sparkling cider."

"She brought sparkling cider up to your room? Are you for real?" She asked with a confused chuckle.

"Yes, why?"

"Maybe you should tell me what happened from the beginning.

John told Sara the entire story of what happened from the beginning to the very end. He told her what happened in the New York airport and in Boston between him and Cheryl.

"Ok, if everything you are telling me is true, she set you up. Either she or somebody else wanted Shaila to see the two of you on that DVD naked emulating sex."

"Jerry said the same thing, but I still don't understand why. Why would someone try to break up my marriage? I've never done anything to anybody."

Sara leaned back on the couch and threw her head back, and let out a laugh. "That son of a bitch. I knew he was up to something."

"Who? Who are you talking about?" He asked, confused.

"John, there's something I need to do." She patted him on the back. "You hang in there. I'll be in touch."

"Sara, where are you going?! What's going on?!" He yelled. "Will somebody please tell me what's going on here?!" He yelled, throwing his hands up in the air frustrated and letting out a sigh.

Chapter 13

Tommy Meadows walked around his office with a headset on talking to a client. That was how he talked to clients. He didn't really need a desk. He hardly ever sat down. He did all his talking standing up walking around with his headset on. He was a brilliant criminal attorney. He was right up with the best criminal attorneys in the country. He was also Shaila's older brother. He was older than Shaila, but younger than Greg. Tommy was a very nice looking man. He stood about five feet eleven inches tall and weighed about 225 lbs. He was big in the upper chest, and he had dark chocolate skin and a bald head.

"I want a divorce, and I want you to draw up the papers," Shaila said as she rushed into his office.

"I need to call you back," he told the person on the other line, and then hung up the phone. "Hello to you too, sis," he said sarcastically.

"I'm sorry, Tommy." She walked over to him and gave him a hug. He motioned for her to have a seat on his couch against the wall.

"Ok, tell me what happened. Why do you want to divorce John?"

"He cheated on me, Tommy."

He sat back on the couch, put his hand on his mouth, and shook his head in disgust. "Damn!" was all he could say. "Did he tell you? How did you find out?"

"Somebody sent me a DVD with him and some woman having sex. I confronted him about it and kicked him out."

"Son of a Bitch! And I thought John was a good person. Shaila, I'm sorry."

"Tommy, I want you to draw up the papers right now. I want out of this marriage."

"Honey, you know I'm not a divorce attorney. I don't specialize in that particular form of law and even if I did, I would advise you to take a couple of days and think about this. You're upset and hurt right now. You're not thinking rationally enough to make that kind of decision."

"Oh my bad, I was under the assumption since you are my brother that you would do this for me. I guess I was wrong. Instead of helping me, you defend him. I thought you, of all people, would be on my side."

"I'm not defending him and I am on your side, but you and John have loved one another for ten years. Did you even give him a chance to explain, or did you go on one of your tirades and not listen to him like you usually do? I really find it hard to believe he would intentionally hurt you like that."

"I have the DVD to prove it. That's all the evidence I need. A picture is worth a thousand words."

"Honey, I'm sorry. I'm not making light of this. Do you want me to talk to him?"

"No, thank you. This is something I have to work out on my own."

"Honey, I wish I had the answers for you. One piece of advice I can give you is talk to John. He owes you an explanation. Make him give you one."

"He tried to explain last night, but I wouldn't listen to him."

"That's understandable. You were too angry to really listen to him. Now that you had some time to cool off, maybe you two can talk. Don't throw it all away until you know what really happened. I'm not saying that will be enough, but at least hear him out. I believe John really does love you. Think about it ok sis."

"Ok, thanks Tommy." She gave him another hug and walked out the door.

As Shaila walked out to her SUV, she felt a little queasy and dizzy. She concluded that she felt that way because she hadn't eaten anything since lunch yesterday afternoon. She really didn't feel like eating, but she really needed to. It was already two o'clock. She decided to get a sandwich and take it home. After thinking about it, she didn't want to go home because she figured John would be there getting the rest of his clothes. She couldn't handle seeing him right now. She decided to go back to the office instead. She took her lunch and went up to her office and shut the door. She sat down at her desk and ate her sandwich.

"Hi, I didn't know you were here. I was going to leave these documents on your desk. Are you ok? You took off so early I thought there was a problem," Sidney inquired.

"Everything's fine, I had some personal business I had to take care of. Did you need me for anything?"

"No, but John was here looking for you. I told him I didn't know where you were."

"What did he say?"

"Well, he was in here talking to Sara for a while. Then Sara ran out of here and left the building. John left soon after."

"Thanks, oh Sidney, will you call down to Luke and let him know I will have the Carlson deposition ready by the end of the day. Thank you."

"I'll do that right now."

Shaila was working on the deposition trying to concentrate when Marc walked in her office. "Hi, how are you doing? I thought you were going home for the day."

"I was, but I decided I needed to get some work done. Besides, what good would it do to go home and wallow in this? I need to stay busy. You know what I mean?"

"Yeah, I know. Have you spoken to John yet?" As soon as he asked her the question, her phone rang. She looked at the caller ID to see John's cell number. She let it ring.

"No, I haven't spoken to him today."

"Was that him who just called?"

"Yes, I can't talk to him right now. I'm afraid of what he's going to say."

"What do you think he's going to say?"

"I want him to say he didn't sleep with another woman, but I know that's not true." Marc felt guilty after hearing what she just said, but not enough to tell her the truth.

"Well, I have to get back to the office. Listen Shaila, would you like to take a drive with me tomorrow to clear your head?"

"Sure, why not?"

"I'll call her tomorrow."

She nodded her head as if to say ok. He left her alone with her work.

Sara was at the library surfing the net for information on Marc. She had found some very interesting things about him. It seemed a couple of years ago he was investigated for misuse of funds, but the investigation was dropped due to lack of evidence. According to the article reports, he was accused of skimming money and moving it from one account to another. He was also investigated for possible arson when his company burned to the ground. He was on the verge of bankruptcy when his company mysteriously burned to the ground. He received a hefty insurance check and he built a bigger and better company. The investigation geared toward Marc, but again they didn't have enough evidence to indict. This information was not going to help her. Nothing came out of the investigations. He wasn't charged with anything. She needed something tangible. She knew Marc had something to do with what happened in Boston.

It was a gut feeling. She never really trusted him. She had met him and talked to him a couple of times after Shaila convinced him to come on board with the firm. He seemed kind of shady to her. It was like he was interested more in what Shaila was doing. Where Shaila was going. Was Shaila here or was Shaila there? He never really was interested in anything but Shaila. His own company's well-being didn't really seem to interest him either, only Shaila. She had to help John and Shaila save their marriage. She left the library, got into her BMW, and drove to Wilson, Inc. She wasn't sure what she would find, but she had to try. She pulled into the parking lot and happened to see Marc getting into his Maserati and driving off. She proceeded to follow him. He drove at a high rate of speed down the interstate, but she kept up with him. She was no slacker when it came to keeping up with New York traffic. He was headed out of the city. After driving for about thirty minutes, he pulled into a condominium complex. He parked his Maserati in front of condo 214 and proceeded to the door. He knocked on the door and a pretty young African American woman opened the door.

"The DVD has been sent and Shaila has seen it," he told Cheryl.

"Have you talked to her?"

"Yes, she poured her heart out to me this afternoon. I have to admit I did feel guilty when she was crying, but it did feel good to hold her in my arms again. That's where she belongs. I think I have a good chance of getting her back."

She nodded her head at him.

"Don't worry, baby, I will still take care of you as long as you do right," he said to her. He lifted her chin and kissed her. She pulled away from him.

"Where are you going? You come back here." She walked back to him "Take off those clothes." He kissed her lips downward to her neck and to her breastbone. He picked her up and carried her to the couch where they made love.

"Where does that leave me when you and Shaila get back together?"

"If you're asking whether or not I will still sleep with you when Shaila and I get back together, the answer is no. Shaila is the one I want. She's the one I've always wanted. I've already made that mistake once. I won't do it again. I will, however, continue to pay for everything per our agreement." He got up and went to the bathroom and washed up. He put his clothes back on, kissed her forehead, and walked out the door. She let out a sigh and went to the bathroom to wash up.

Sara waited in her car for about an hour before she saw Marc come out of the condo. He got into his Maserati and drove away. She got out of her car and walked up to the door Marc had just come out of. She knocked on the door, and Cheryl answered.

"Hi, can I help you?"

"Hi, I'm looking for Allison Sampson. Does she live here? I was told this was her address." Sara asked.

"No, she doesn't."

"I'm sorry, I could have sworn this was the address she gave me. This is 214 E. Hanson, isn't it?"

"No, this is 214 E. Emerson."

"I feel so foolish. I can't believe I came to the wrong address. Where are my manners?" She extended her hand to Cheryl. "My name is Emily Woodard. May I ask your name? Would you listen to me? I'm being way too personal. I'm sorry. I just like to put a name with the face. I guess it's the small town girl in me," she said with a chuckle. "Where I'm from everyone knows everyone. I have to remember I'm in a big city now. I can't do that anymore. Nowadays, people will shoot you for no reason. I have to remember I can't just come up to anybody and start a conversation. It's going to take some time to get used to.

"Yeah, I know what you mean. My name is Cheryl, Cheryl Crosby." She shook Sara's hand.

"Well, It was a pleasure meeting you Miss Crosby. I apologize for disturbing you."

"No problem."

Sara turned and walked to her car. "Gotcha," she said with a smile. "Damn, I'm good.

Chapter 14

John sat at his desk at work looking over his test results. All his tests came back negative. He had Jerry run every test known to man and put a rush on them. Jerry anxiously complied because he too wanted to make sure John was alright. John wanted to make sure if he had sex with Cheryl that he didn't contract some disease. Jerry, being John's friend, did the tests himself and promised to keep it between the two of them. Although the tests came up negative, John would have to get tested periodically to make sure nothing popped up in the future. Even though John knew in his heart he didn't sleep with that woman, he still had to play it safe. He racked his brain trying to figure out who would be so devious as to set him up like that, but no one came to mind. He didn't have any enemies he could conceive of. It just didn't make sense. John sat in his leather chair with his head back and his legs stretched out in front of him when he looked up to see Greg standing in front of him.

Greg was a nice looking man. He stood five feet ten inches, and weighed 185 lbs. He was light skinned with a small mustache and goatee, brown eyes and short hair cut.

"I've heard everything there is to hear on the subject. If I knew what happened in Boston, believe me I would tell everyone, but I don't know what happened. So if you're here to ream me a new one, save your breath, ok. You can't make me feel worse than I already do," John said.

"Did you drink so much that you didn't remember sleeping with another woman behind my sister's back? You couldn't come up with a better lie than I don't remember? I thought you were smarter than that. When Tommy told me you cheated on Shaila, I thought to myself there's no way in hell John would do that to her, He loves her too much, then he told me about the DVD."

John sat in his chair with his hands clasped together in front of him swinging side to side. He seemed calm, cool, and collected on the outside, but he was falling apart on the inside. "Tell me something, Greg, did you actually see the DVD?"

"Are you saying there is no DVD?"

"No, there's a DVD, and I'm in it clear as day. There's no disputing that."

"You took vows to love, honor, and cherish my sister til death do you part and yet you humiliate her by sleeping with another woman. Just tell me why, why did you cheat on my sister?"

"I can sit here and try to explain myself until I'm blue in the face, but you won't believe a word I say, and I don't blame you. I really don't. If I were in your shoes. I wouldn't believe me either. I'm just going to have to prove to everyone, especially Shaila, I'm not the cheating bastard everyone thinks I am."

"John, if it were anybody else besides you sitting in that chair, I would have come in here and knocked the hell out of him, but I still think you are a good man despite what may and may not have happened in Boston. I'm not saying you didn't do anything and I'm not saying you did, but if there is a good explanation for why you are on this DVD naked with a naked woman on top of you, you better figure it out real quick. You feel me?"

"I feel you."

"Good, just so we're clear."

Sara had all the information on Cheryl to take back to John, but she really wanted to get something on Marc to take back to him as well, but Marc had a lot of high-powered connections that seemed to get him out of a lot of jams. Sara was digging into his past businesses, but like before nothing came that was tangible so she decided to look into his personal life. This guy was dirty. She could feel it. She just had to find out his dirty deeds. Her friend's marriage depended on it. As Sara was surfing the net, she found something very strange. There was not one piece of information on Marc Wilson with his social security number before the age of 18 years old. It was like he was born at 18 years old. Sara did a little more digging. Sara was a whiz at finding facts on the internet. She could find just about anything on anybody. After about an hour of surfing the net, she came up with something very shocking. "Oh my God!"

She copied the information onto two discs. She copied the information on two discs just in case if something happened to the original disc, she would have a back up. She put one copy in her briefcase and another copy in her pantsuit pocket. She grabbed her purse and raced to her car. She had to get the information she had discovered over to John now. She unlocked her car with her remote and threw her purse and her briefcase onto her passenger seat.

"Why were you following me yesterday?" Marc asked, startling her.

Sara turned around with such a startled movement she dropped her keys on the ground.

Marc leaned down and picked them up for her.

"What do you mean?"

"Oh come on, I noticed your car in the parking lot as I got into my Maserati and drove away. I also noticed you following me. You followed me all the way to Cheryl's condo. I saw you pull in behind me and park on the opposite side of the street. You're not very discreet. You were following so closely I could see your face in the rearview mirror. So I will ask you again, " Why were you following me?"

"For the last time, I wasn't following you, and I don't have a clue who Cheryl is."

"To be an attorney, you really aren't a good liar."

Sara stood in front of Marc scared to death. She did know his secret and she didn't know what he would do to her to keep it quiet.

She had to figure out a way to get him away from her so she could get into her car and leave. "I don't know what you're talking about so if you would excuse me, I have to go." She tried to turn around to get into her car, but Marc grabbed her arm.

"Let's cut the crap shall we? I want what's in your briefcase."

"What makes you think that I have anything in there that pertains to you?"

"Sara, Sara, Sara, why couldn't you just mind your own business? This complicates things for me."

Sara's heart beat so rapidly she felt it would burst out of her chest. Her breathing was more finite and was shaking uncontrollably. "You're not going to get away with this. Eventually all of what you have done will catch up with you."

"Maybe, maybe not, but you won't be the one telling my secrets." He reached into his jacket pocket and pulled out a stun gun and shocked her. She fell limp into his arms. He looked around to make sure no one was around, and picked her up and laid her in the back seat of her car. He took out his gloves and put them on. He took his handkerchief and wiped the fingerprints off her door handle. He proceeded into the driver's seat, looked into her briefcase, found the disc and put it into his left inside jacket pocket. He looked in her purse to find her address on her driver's license. He drove her car out of the parking lot and proceeded to Sara's house.

He pulled into the parking garage of her building and parked her car in her designated parking spot. He got out and looked around to make sure nobody was around to see him take her out of the back seat. He picked her up and carried her up to her apartment. Fortunately, no one was around to see him carrying her. He unlocked her door to her apartment and took her inside. He laid her on the couch, grabbed a pillow from the couch, and placed it over her face. The effects of the stun gun had worn off because she started to struggle trying to get air into her lungs. He pressed the pillow harder and harder into her face until she stopped breathing. This went on for about three minutes. After having to go through the struggle of killing her, he was tired trying to catch his breath. He put the pillow back into its original place on the couch. He checked her pulse to make sure she was dead. He left her lifeless body on the couch. Marc had killed Sara to keep his secret safe. He positioned her body on her side to make it look like she died in her sleep. Unfortunately for him. He didn't realize the other disc she had copied was in the pocket he had laid her on. He took a small plastic bag full of cocaine and spread some of it out and chopped it up into lines on her coffee table. He placed a tightly round dollar bill on the table to make it look like she had been snorting cocaine. He took his cell phone out of his jacket pocket and dialed a number. "Hi, I'm on my way, be ready for an adventure."

"Where are we going?" "Shaila asked.

"It's a surprise. I want to take you somewhere special to get your mind off your problems."

"Are you going to tell me, or do I have to guess?"

"Well, if I tell you, it won't be a surprise now will it?"

"No, I guess not."

He drove to a private airport where his private jet was fueled and ready to go. "Here we are. Come on."

"Wait, I can't just pick up and jet off somewhere. I do have a job," Shaila said.

"Oh come on, live a little. Besides, it's Friday. You don't have to be back at work until Monday."

"I didn't pack anything to take with me. All I have is what I'm wearing."

"I'll buy you whatever you need when we get there. Now come on."

They boarded the plane which was like a hotel suite. It had two couches across from each other and two loveseats with a big black lacquer table sitting in the middle. Shaila had bought extravagant things of her own, but nothing like that. She was amazed.

"Marc, this is beautiful. This is a hotel suite, not a plane. When you said you wanted to take me for a ride, I was actually thinking it would be in your car. Not that I'm complaining, but you still haven't told me where we're going."

"Like I said, you will find out soon enough. Relax and enjoy the trip. You'll love it. Excuse me, I need to check on something."

"Sure."

Marc came back into the room with a tray of food. The plate had a round silver top over it. He had a white towel over his arm like a waiter wears at an elegant party. "For you madam," he said in a snooty, but funny voice.

"What's this?" She asked with a smile.

He put the tray down in front of her and lifted the top off the china. On the plate was fettuccine alfredo with crab meat dipped in creamy sauce, and parmesan cheese sprinkled on top. To the side sat a tall glass of coke with cherry grenadine and a cherry just the way she liked it. Sitting on the other side of the plate sat a small but elegant vase with a single and flawless lavender rose in water. She was so touched that he remembered her favorite food and drink.

"I can't believe you remembered all of this, thank you." Just then a small tear fell down her cheek.

"Baby please don't cry," he leaned down and wiped away the tears.

"I'm ok. What about you? Aren't you going to eat something? I don't want to eat by myself."

The waiter brought in another tray for Marc and sat it down in front of him. He had the same only he had a glass of champagne to drink. He didn't offer her any champagne because he knew she didn't drink all that much. They ate their food and talked while awaiting their arrival to wherever they were going. Only Marc and the pilots knew that little secret. The waiter came back in to take their trays away, and asked if there was anything else he could do for them. They both said no thank you. He nodded, turned and walked out of the room.

"Marc, we have been flying for hours. Where are we?"

"We're almost there, just be patient. I'll go see where we are." He came back and told her to put her seatbelt on because they would be landing in twenty minutes.

When the plane landed. The doors opened, they climbed down the stairs, and to Shaila's surprise Marc had his pilots fly them to Cancun. There was a limo waiting for them outside the airport. The driver took them to the very hotel they stayed in college when they went on spring break. They walked into the hotel and the manager came up to Marc and greeted him as if he owned the place, which to Shaila's surprise, he did. He bought it three years earlier.

"You bought this place?"

"Yeah I did."

"When?"

"About three years ago. It was a good investment. I couldn't pass it up."

"I can't believe you did this. You're full of surprises."

"Come on, let's go to the suites. Don't worry. We have separate suites. We have the whole floor to ourselves. Everything you need is up in your suite.

They rode the elevator up to the twelfth floor. Shaila took her card key and unlocked her door. She walked in to find the most spectacular room she had ever seen. The suite had three bedrooms with three full baths in each room. Each room had a king-sized bed with a leather sofa and loveseats to match. The faucets were made of gold and the tile was a flawless white. The bathroom had a whirlpool bathtub and a picture window overlooking the beach and ocean. The kitchen was just the right size. It was equipped with a stove, refrigerator, microwave and dishwasher. The cabinets were stocked with all the finest china. Everything in the place was brand new. Marc had gone all out when he bought the place years ago. In the living room sat an L shaped couch with a loveseat to match and a built in reclining chair. The balcony had a beautiful view of the ocean. You could see as far out as the sunset. The balcony had a wet bar stocked full of every drink one could imagine.

Shaila went into the master suite and opened the closet door to find every kind of clothes in her size she could imagine. Marc said he had taken care of everything and he did. As she took in the beauty of the suite, there was a knock on the door. She opened the door. "Marc, this is spectacular."

"Thank you. I had it decorated mostly per your taste. You always had exquisite taste. I was hoping you would like it."

"I love it, and the clothes they're beautiful. One question, do you plan on holding me hostage?"

"Well, I thought about it," he laughed. "I wasn't sure what you would need so I bought everything you liked to wear. You can keep everything. They are specifically made for you. I just hope I remembered the right size."

"You did, thank you."

"Get dressed. I'm taking you out dancing tonight. I know how much you love to dance. I'll be back to get you in an hour. Will that be enough time for you to get ready?"

"That will be more than enough time."

Shaila went into the closet and looked through all the clothes trying to decide which one she was going to wear that evening. She finally chose a form-fitted strapless red sequined dress with matching red pumps. She laid the dress out on the bed along with a beautiful pair of sapphire earrings and necklace. She went in to take a quick shower. She got out of the shower and put on her makeup, put her hair up into an upswept style on top of her head. It had curls that fell down her neck. She looked absolutely stunning. She was ready for her night of dancing and she wasn't going to let any of her problems come to the surface, not tonight.

Marc came to the door a perfect gentleman. He had come bearing a dozen lavender roses and chocolate candies. He really went all out to impress her. He had to get her to forget all about John. That was the plan. She took the roses and put them in water and set them on the dining room table.

"Thank you. They're so beautiful."

"Beautiful roses for a beautiful lady. You look absolutely stunning. Are you ready to go?"

"Yes."

He lifted his arm and Shaila took hold by putting her arm around his. They took the elevator to the lobby. As they stepped out of the elevator, all eyes were on the beautiful couple. Marc wore a dark gray pinstripe suit, and black tie, and shoes. They were definitely dressed to impress. They had the look and they wore it well. They really did compliment each other. When they reached outside there was a black stretched Mercedes limo waiting for them. The doorman opened the door and Shaila slid into the seat. Marc slid in after he had given the doorman a very handsome tip. In the limo there was candlelight and soft music playing in the background.

"Where are we going?"

"To a nice, respectable club down the street. You'll love the dancing and the scenery. You'll love the music, trust me."

When they arrived at the club, there was a long line to get in. Marc shook hands and nodded to several people standing in line and walked in with Shaila by his side. The hostess greeted the couple and sat them in the VIP section. Already sitting on the table was a bottle of the finest champagne chilling in a bucket of ice.

"Is there anything you don't own?" She asked.

"I don't own the beach, but it wasn't from the lack of trying."

They both laughed then Marc graciously excused himself from the table. Shaila sat at the boot taken in the scenery when all of sudden Marc came back over and sat down beside her.

"Where did you go?"

"I had to make sure everything was in place."

"What did you do?"

"You'll see. Just wait."

The lights became very dim and music started playing. It was Shaila's favorite song. As she was sitting in the booth swaying to the sound of the music, Marc told her to turn around. Standing behind her was Patti Labelle singing If Only You Knew. She was completely shocked. She couldn't believe Marc surprised her with Patti right in front of her singing her favorite song. She began to cry. Her voice was so smooth and heavenly. It literally made her weak in the knees. She sang a couple of songs to her. When Patti was done, everyone in the place gave her a standing ovation. She hugged Shaila and said goodbye. She was happy and tearful all at the same time. She said thank you while Patti kissed Marc on the cheek.

"Marc, h–how did you do this? How did you get Patti Labelle to come and sing at your club?"

"A friend of mine knows her agent. He hooked me up."

"You had all of this planned from the start, didn't you?"

"Maybe," he answered coyly.

She wrapped her arms around his neck and gave him a hug and a kiss on the cheek. The rest of the night they danced the night away in each other's arms.

It was the wee hours of the morning when they got back to the hotel. Marc walked her to her suite. He looked deep into her eyes and leaned his head down to give her a kiss. Shaila knew she shouldn't because she was a married woman, but temptation overwhelmed her. They stood in front of her door and tasted each other for what seemed like a lifetime. She broke off the kiss and told him good night. She took the keycard and slid it through the lock and let herself in. She waved goodbye to him and closed the door behind her. She leaned up against the door and smiled. Marc grinned and turned around and headed back to his own suite.

Shaila woke up the next morning confused. She had a great time with Marc the night before, but she felt guilty about the kiss they shared. Even though it didn't go any further than that, she felt like she just cheated on her husband. How could she stop herself if it happened again? She couldn't give into her feelings for Marc. She got out of bed and went into the kitchen to make herself a cup of tea. She placed the kettle full of water on the burner to boil. There was a knock at the door, and she knew it was Marc. She gave herself a once over in the mirror before opening the door. What she saw in the mirror didn't look too bad at all. She answered the door with nothing but a silk nightgown and matching robe. Standing on the other side of the door was Marc wearing blue jean shorts and a white buttoned down pressed shirt.

"Hi," she said.

"Hi, can I come in?"

"Sure." She stepped out of the way to let him in.

"I wanted to let you know I had a great time with you last night," he said.

"I did too."

"Look, about the kiss, I got a little carried away and I'm sorry. I shouldn't have kissed you."

"No, Marc. it's ok I was there too. It wasn't just you. I wanted it just as much as you did. Let's just leave it at that."

"Good, I'm glad you bear no hard feelings. How about breakfast? I don't know about you, but I'm starving."

"Me too. Let me get dressed and then we can go."

Shaila went into the kitchen and turned off the tea and then she went into the bedroom and threw on a light blue sundress and matching sandals. She went into the bathroom and brushed her teeth, cleaned up, and came out ready to go.

"You look beautiful. Are you ready to go?"

"Yeah, I'm ready."

They spent the day shopping, walking along the beach, and talking about their lives and careers. They were so in sync with each other it was almost scary. It was like they were a couple, but they weren't. Walking along the beach, Shaila had her sandals in one hand and Marc's hand in the other. They stopped to look at the sunset over the blue water. They sat down and she leaned her head on his shoulder.

"This is amazing," she said.

"What is?"

"Being here with you again, everything."

"You're the one who's amazing. After all these years, you take my breath away."

She looked up into his green eyes and caressed his cheek with the back of her hand. He put his hand on top of hers and leaned over and kissed her. He laid on top of her, her head in the sand and kissed her passionately. She tried not to succumb to desire, but the desire within her was overwhelming. He caressed every inch of her kissing with all the desire he had inside of him. Deep down she knew she shouldn't succumb to passion, but at that point she really didn't care. Her body needed this.

"Take me upstairs."

"Are you sure about this?" He asked.

"I'm very sure."

"I don't want to pressure you into anything. That's not what this is about."

"I know this is what I want."

He picked her up and carried her up to his suite. He laid her on his bed and began to undress her. He kissed every inch of her. He stopped and took a condom from the night stand and slid it over his erection. He slowly entered her and began to make love to her like it was their first time. They found ecstasy in each other's arms. Marc realized when he removed the condom that it had broken, but he didn't tell her. He took the condom and threw it in the trash can. She laid her head on his chest and fell asleep.

Chapter 15

It was Sunday morning. The sun shined bright and the ocean waves slammed against the beach. Marc woke up to find Shaila asleep in his arms. He pushed the strands of her hair away from her face, and she began to stir.

"Good morning," he said.

She smiled and said, "good morning."

"How'd you sleep?"

"Like a baby. I always sleep like a baby in your arms."

He looked at her with his intense green eyes. "Last night was amazing. It felt so good, so right. I have waited for that moment since the day we had lunch at La Maison. I'd love to stay here with you forever, but we have to get ready to go, and get back to the real world. I'll call and make sure the jet is fueled and ready to go." He got up naked as the day he was born, and she loved the view. God, this man was gorgeous. He walked towards the bathroom, and she followed close behind putting her arms around his waist and gave him a hug. He turned to her and lifted her chin up to meet his gaze and kissed her.

"Do we have to go now? I'm not ready to go back."

"I'm afraid so. I'm going to make sure everything's in order. You pack your stuff." He turned and began to walk away. She told him to stop. He turned and walked back to her. She jumped into his arms and hugged him as if they were one.

"I don't want this weekend to end."

"Neither do I, but we have to work tomorrow, and I can't keep you here forever. Although, I wish I could." He looked at her, like he wanted to say something to her, but decided against it. As he began to turn and walk away, he quickly changed his mind and turned towards her. He pulled her into his arms and held her tightly. "I want to tell you something you probably already know, but I have to say it. I love you, Shaila. I knew I loved you, but I didn't know how much until we made love last night. You and I belong together, and I think you agree with me. You couldn't make love to me the way you did last night and not feel something. Look, I know you still have to deal with Jon, and I understand that, but I know you can't look me in the eye and tell me you don't feel something for me. "I'm going to wait for you no matter how long it takes." He turned and walked away leaving her standing alone thinking about what he just told her.

Shaila got home Sunday evening. She had a wonderful weekend with Marc. She really needed to get away and think things through, but now she was more confused than ever. What were her feelings for Marc? Did she love him like he loved her? She went upstairs to her bedroom, and looked into the closet that she and John once shared to find his side of the closet totally cleaned out. He was gone. She let out a sigh and walked over and sat down on the bed. She noticed she had messages on her answering machine. She pressed play to listen to her messages. There was one from her mother asking how she was doing and to call her when she got a minute. Greg and Tommy both left messages and John had left four messages asking her to please call back, and that he missed and loved her. The bizarre message was from Ben asking if she had heard from Sara. He said Sara didn't come to work Friday afternoon and no one could get her at home or on her cell phone. Shaila immediately called Ben at home.

"Hello," he answered.

"Hey Ben, It's Shaila. I just got your message. Have you heard from Sara yet?"

"No, and I'm getting worried. That's why I called you. You know her better than anyone. Where could she be?"

"I don't know. Did you go by her apartment?"

"No, not yet."

"I will. I have a key. She gave me a key in case of an emergency. I'm sure she's fine, but I'm going over there just to make sure nothing's wrong."

"Call me when you find out something. Everyone is worried about her." "I will. Goodbye Ben."

"Goodbye."

Shaila picked up her keys to her SUV along with her purse and ran down the stairs. She opened the front door to find John standing on the other side of the door getting ready to knock.

"John, what are you doing here?"

"I was hoping we could talk."

"We need to talk, but right now is not a good time. I have to go find Sara."

"What's wrong with Sara? Is she hurt?"

"I don't know, probably not, it's just that no one has heard from her since Friday morning."

"Do you mind if I come with you? I want to make sure she's ok as well."

"Yeah, come on."

Shaila and John walked up to Sara's apartment and knocked on the door. There was no answer. John knocked even louder, still no answer. They knew she was there because her car was in the parking garage. Shaila took her key and let the two of them into the apartment. She and John found Sara lying on the couch with drugs all over the coffee table. Sara went into emergency mode. She ran over and checked her pulse, but she was cold and blue. "Oh my God, John, call 911." She immediately tried to administer CPR. The 911 dispatcher dispatched the ambulance and the police to Sara's address.

John could tell she was already dead because she was blue and stiff. "Baby, she's gone." He went over to Shaila and pulled her up into his arms. Shaila immediately broke down crying. Finally, after what seemed like a lifetime, the paramedics along with the police showed up on the scene. The paramedics tried to revive her the same as Shaila, but it was too late. Sara had been dead for two days. Since the day Marc had smothered her with a pillow. She was pronounced dead at the scene. Shaila shuddered and cried uncontrollably in John's arms. She went over to the chair and sat down with her knees up to her chest and sobbed. John immediately knelt in front of her and rubbed the back of her hair.

"I'm so sorry, baby." She put her knees down and hugged him with all the strength she had. All her fear, anger, hurt, and sadness came pouring out in tears. "Let it out, baby. Let it all out." He held her tightly to comfort her. The Detective came over to talk to them.

"Excuse me ma'am, did you know the deceased?"

Shaila shook her head yes. "She was a Litigator in my law firm, and a good friend. We worked together at York, Anderson, and Locke. Her name was Sara Jones."

He took down some notes in his notepad. "Did you ever suspect she had a drug problem?"

"No, she's never had a drug problem. As a matter of fact, she was dead set against drugs. I know there are drugs all over the place, and I know what you're thinking, but she wouldn't OD on drugs. She wouldn't have killed herself either."

"Do you know anyone who would want to harm Miss Jones? Any jealous boyfriends or clients who were harassing her? Was she depressed?"

"No, not that I know of. She got along with everyone, and she didn't seem depressed to me. Actually, she was very happy. She was doing well at her job. As a matter of fact, we were working on a case together. Everything seemed fine."

"What made you come over to check on her?"

"She never made it back to the office Friday after lunch, and everyone was worried when no one could get a hold of her?"

"What made you wait until this evening to come and check on her?"

"I just got back into town about an hour ago. That's when I checked my messages. Ben had called and left a message asking if I had seen her. I immediately called him, and he told me no one had heard from her since Friday. I told him I had a key to her apartment, and I would come over and check on her. John and I found her like this. I tried to give her CPR, but nothing."

John wondered where Shaila had been and why she was just getting back into town, but he didn't say anything about it. He would ask about it later.

"Ok, thank you for your information. If I have any more questions, I will be in touch. Here is my card in case you remember anything else. I'm sorry for your loss."

When the medical examiner moved Sara's body to transfer her to the gurney, a black disc dropped out of her pocket. No one noticed it except John. Everyone else was focused on other things. Shaila was even too distraught to notice. John walked over to where the disc fell and picked it up and put it in his back pocket. He wasn't exactly sure what was on the disc, but he took it just in case it might have something on it that could hurt Sara's reputation, and he didn't want anyone to see it until he had a chance to review it. He knew enough about the law from Shaila that he could get into serious trouble for tampering with evidence, but he didn't really care at this moment.

John walked over to Shaila and put his arm around her and asked her if she was ready to go home. She nodded yes. She gave him the keys to her SUV and he drove her back to the penthouse. She walked into her house with John not far behind. She walked into the den and dialed Ben's home phone number. When he answered, Shaila told him through tears she and John found her dead in her apartment. He was completely floored, and he felt guilty because he should have checked on her sooner. He was so distraught he could barely talk. He cried while he was on the phone with her. They both agreed they would tell everyone at the office the next day. She said goodbye and hung up the phone.

"Do you want me to make you some tea? It might calm you."

She shook her head no.

"Is there anyone I can call on Sara's behalf? Any family anywhere?"

"No, her parents were killed in a car accident and she didn't have any brothers or sisters. She didn't have anyone."

"She had you. You were a great friend to her."

"Why, why did this happen?" She cried in John's arms..

"I don't know, baby. I don't know."

"John, will you stay with me tonight? I really don't want to be alone."

This was exactly what he wanted to hear from his beloved. He was thrilled she asked him to stay. "Of course I will. I will stay as long as you need me to. Are you hungry? Would you like me to fix you something to eat?"

"No, thank you."

They sat on the couch and held each other until Shaila fell asleep in his arms. John carried her upstairs to the bedroom they used to share and laid her down. He took her shoes off and put them to the side of the bed. He gently put the covers over top of her, laid down next to her and watched her sleep.

Chapter 16

After Shaila and Ben broke the news to everyone about Sara's death, the entire office was very sad and grief stricken. It was impossible to believe Sara was truly gone. There wasn't a dry eye in the place. Ben had asked that all the assistants reschedule all the appointments for the day. He insisted that everyone go home for the day and try to find some peace. He and Shaila had arranged for grief counseling for anyone who wanted to talk. The counselors were available at any time. This was the time to spend with family. They were not to come back until the next day. Sara's colleagues needed time to grieve for her. Shaila also wanted to let everyone know the office would also be shut down so everyone could attend the funeral. She would let everyone know the funeral arrangements once she had them completed.

Shaila decided she would arrange the funeral since Sara had no family, and she wanted to do right by her friend.

Shaila came home to a ringing telephone, but she didn't answer. She let it go to voicemail. She didn't feel like talking to anybody at the moment. She heard Marc's voice when he left a message on her voicemail.

"Shaila, it's Marc. I just heard about Sara and I wanted to tell you how sorry I am. If you need to talk, call me. Love you, bye."

Sara sat on the couch in her den with her head resting on the back of the couch. She was alone in her penthouse in the middle of the day. She had mixed feelings. She didn't want to be around anyone, but she didn't want to be alone either. She was confused. She missed her friend and confidant. She sat on her couch and wept some more. She had cried so many tears that she thought there couldn't possibly be any left to cry, but she was wrong. They flowed like Niagra Falls. The doorbell rang, and Shaila begrudgingly got up to answer the door. Jasmine walked in the door and instantly gave Shaila a hug.

"John asked if I would come over and check on you. He's really worried about you. He would have come himself, but he didn't want to upset you more. How are you holding up?"

"I'm ok, I guess. I don't think it has really sunk in yet, you know? John and I found her, so I know she's really gone, but it's like it isn't true. You know what I mean?"

"Yeah, I know. Did they find out how she died?"

"I don't think so, but I don't know. I haven't heard anything. I'm assuming they'll do an autopsy because she died under mysterious circumstances."

"What do you think they will find?"

She shrugged. "I don't know. On one hand, I want them to find drugs in her system. At least then we would know it really was a drug overdose and that would be the end of it. On the other hand, if there aren't any traces of drugs in her system, then that would probably mean there was foul play, but it would exonerate her from being a junkie. God, how could this have happened? I just don't understand."

"I wish there was something I could do or say to make it all better. I'm so sorry. I really am."

"I know thank you. Let's talk about something else for the time being. This topic has been on my mind since John and I found her last night."

"Ok, what's going on with you and John?" She asked probing for details.

"Well, damn, let's not beat around the bush. Let's just come right out with it. Don't be shy."

"I'm serious, Shaila, what's going on?"

"There isn't really much to say. We haven't sat down and talked about it yet. I guess I'm kind of afraid to really sit down and talk to him. When it comes right down to it, I'm not as strong as everyone thinks I am."

"You didn't get to where you are by being gullible and weak. You're a lot stronger than you give yourself credit for." She sat back in her chair, crossed her legs by the knee and gave out a sigh. "Shaila, I want to ask you something important, and I want you to tell me the truth."

"Ok."

"Do you still love John?"

Rubbing the sides of her temple she contemplated the question Jasmine just asked. "Honestly, yes, I love John more than anything."

"You haven't even given him the opportunity to at least try to explain, but yet you're ready to write him off like you never loved him. Is that fair? You could at least give him the benefit of the doubt. You two have been together for a long time. You don't want to throw it all away without talking about what happened. You two really need to clear the air."

"There's a little bit more to it than that."

"What do you mean?" Jasmine asked with a puzzled look on her face.

"There is the issue of Marc."

"Marc? What does Marc have to do with what happened between you and John?"

"I went to Mexico with him this past weekend, and one thing led to another, and we, we slept together."

Jasmine shook her head in disbelief and let out a sigh. Of all the people that would cheat on each other, she never would have guessed it would have been John and Shaila. They seemed to have the perfect marriage. At least that was what everyone thought, but no one knew what went on behind closed doors. She was totally blindsided by this turn of events, and she really didn't know what to say to Shaila's admittance. "Shaila, you didn't. Two wrongs don't make it right."

"I know. I know. Maybe I wanted to get back at John. I am so confused."

"Do you love Marc?"

"I know I feel something, but I don't know if it's love. I do know it wasn't just sex. There was a lot more to it than that."

"Are you going to tell John?"

"I guess I should. That would be the right thing to do."

"I guess it would be." She gave Shaila a look like she had something else she wanted to say. "What?" Shaila finally asked.

"Oh, I was just wondering why John would invite a strange woman into his hotel room and let her videotape him and her having sex knowing it would get back to you. Something to think about, don't you think?"

"Are you suggesting John didn't cheat on me?"

"I'm not suggesting anything. You're the one with the disc. You tell me. It might not hurt to take a closer look. Personally, I haven't seen the disc, but video images can be altered. People do it all the time. All I'm saying is it might benefit you to take another look."

She sat up and walked over to Shaila and brought her into a hug. "I know this is a very difficult time for you right now, and you and John are going through a rough patch right now, and whatever happened with him and that woman, and you and Marc, that's between you two. I love you, sis, and all I want is for you to be happy. Whatever you decide to do, will be your decision. I won't say anything about what happened between you and Marc. That's your story to tell, but I strongly urge you to tell John the truth. He deserves that much." She got up and took Shaila's hand into her own. "I love you, sis. You call me if you need anything, ok?"

She nodded. "I love you, too, and thank you."

She let out a deep sigh and decided she was going to tell John everything about Marc, everything. What Jasmine said about the disc made her think. Oh God, what if he really didn't have sex with that woman? What if it was all a set up? That meant that she made a huge mistake and cheated on her husband with no reason to do so. That could mean the end of her marriage, and that's something she would have to live with. She could very well lose her husband and his love. She was so controlled by hurt. It was all consuming, but thinking back she never gave him a chance to explain. She just knew he cheated, but now she was having second thoughts. Could Jasmine be right? Could the disc have been altered? There's only one way to find out.

Shortly after Jasmine left, Shaila went to the shelf where she kept the DVD's and picked up the disc and reluctantly put it in the DVD player. She really didn't want to see the image of John on that disc with another woman. It broke her heart when she first saw it. She sucked it up and pressed play and began watching the disc. At first she couldn't see anything but her husband having sex with another woman, but she kept watching and rewinding, watching and rewinding. She did that for what seemed like hours. She tried to find something, anything that would tell her whether the disc was fake or the real thing. After careful scrutiny of the disc, she realized John was passed out cold. He didn't have sex with her after all.

"My God," she thought to herself. He was set up. He never slept with that woman. He was telling the truth. She sat back on the couch and started to cry. "What have I done?" She was mortified. She had gone away with Marc and slept with him. She had to make things right. She jumped up from the couch, grabbed her purse, and made her way to her SUV. Before she knew it, she was on the elevator on her way to John's office. She stepped out of the elevator and made a beeline to his office.

John sat in his office charting when he looked up to see Shaila standing in the doorway. He immediately jumped up from his chair and walked over to her. She put her hand up to his lips as if to tell him not to say a word.

"I realized something today." she said to him. "I've watched and rewatched that disc, and I realized something I didn't notice before. John, you were passed out."

"Excuse me?" He asked with a puzzled look on his face.

"You were passed out. You weren't moving in the disc. She set you up." Her eyes welled up with tears. He moved closer to her, but she said, "stop, I need you to know. I realized viewing the disc you didn't have sex with that woman. You were passed out cold. She was doing all the work. I watched it over and over today and I realized you were set up. I can't figure out why, but you were definitely set up." The tears fell from her eyes. "I am so sorry. I put you through all of that misery. I didn't believe or trust in you. I have made a mess of everything. Please forgive me."

He pulled her into his arms and said, "there's nothing to forgive. I love you. I'm just glad you finally saw the truth. I have been in pure agony for weeks now. I have thought of nothing but you since we split up."

"John, I need to tell you something, and you may never forgive me, but you need to know." She was about to tell him about her sleeping with Marc. If they were going to make a new start with no secrets, he needed to know everything. Even if it meant she would lose him forever.

"Whatever it is I don't want to know. We were split up for weeks and I don't want to know. Do you love me?"

"Yes, I never stopped."

"Do you want this marriage to work?"

"Yes, more than anything," she cried.

He put his hand on her mouth. "That's all I need to know."

"But, baby, I"

"No." He had a feeling, but he didn't want to hear it. He just wanted his wife back.

Chapter 17

"Here's the report from Sara Jones' autopsy. The autopsy report states that Sara's death was due to asphyxiation. She was probably smothered by a pillow. The report showed there was fabric in her mouth. It could be from someone holding a pillow over her face and her struggling for air, but the interesting thing is, the toxicology result found no drugs in her system whatsoever. She didn't even have aspirin in her system. She was completely clean. Her time of death was between three and five pm. This wasn't an accident or suicide. She was murdered. Someone wanted to make it look like a drug overdose." Detective Jacobs said.

"Yeah, I'm beginning to think you're right. Looking into her background and finances, there's nothing that would suggest she was involved with drugs or anything else nefarious. She was clean. It looked like to me the drugs were staged for our benefit. That was my first thought when I first arrived on scene. It seemed staged, and now the toxicology report just confirmed it. There is no doubt in my mind someone helped her along. Come on let's go," Detective Richards picked up his coat off the back of his chair and put it on.

"Where are we going?"

"We're going fishing, partner. We're going fishing."

HER DANGEROUS LOVER

After seeing the news, Cheryl was shocked. She saw a picture on the news of a woman who had supposedly died of a drug overdose. The woman on television looked a lot like the woman who came to her door a couple of weeks ago claiming she was lost. The woman who came to her door was not Sara Jones like the news said. She remembered her name as Emily Woodward. Maybe it was just a coincidence. Maybe it just looked like the same woman. She thought to herself. Cheryl was deep into the news story when she heard a knock on the door. She got up and answered the door. Marc stood on the other side. She let him in and proceeded back to sit on the couch to continue to watch the news story.

"What's got you so intrigued on that television that you couldn't give me a proper greeting?

"I'm watching a news story about a woman that was found dead in her apartment. She looks a lot like the woman who came to my door a couple of weeks ago claiming to be lost, but this woman they're talking about on the news was named Sara Jones, but she introduced herself as Emily Woodward. I know it's the same woman. I just don't understand why she would claim to be someone she wasn't. Why would she lie to me? I didn't even know her."

"Her name was Sara Jones. She was a Litigator at Shaila's firm. She followed me over here that day. As soon as I left, she came to your door claiming to be lost. My guess is she wanted to find out who you were so she could help John. You must have told her your name. You really are stupid. Why would you tell her your name?"

"How in the hell was I supposed to know who she was, or why she was here? My name is not Sylvia Brown. I'm not a goddamn psychic. For all I knew, she really did get the addresses mixed up and she ended up here. Who did she follow to get here, huh? It sure as hell wasn't me. I don't drive a Maserati," she said furiously.

"Well, it doesn't matter anyway. I took care of it."

"What do you mean you took care of it?"

Marc cocked his head to one side and gave her a knowing look.

"Oh my God, you killed her." She put her hand on her mouth and turned her back to him and walked to the window. She turned back around and faced him. "Have you completely lost your mind? What the hell were you thinking?"

"Would you relax? I made it look like a drug overdose. Nobody will be the wiser. Besides, she found out about my past. I couldn't have her telling John or anybody else. She would have ruined me. I will not go to prison. I had to shut her up. If she would have minded her own business, she would still be alive today. I did what I had to do, and I'm not going to apologize for it."

"Marc, this has gone way too far. You never said anything about killing anyone. I never agreed to murder. What if the police find out? What if they start poking around and find something. A woman is dead because of us. Do you hear me? I don't think I can deal with this."

"You better deal with this, because if you say anything to anybody, I will make sure you go down, and you go down hard," he said with venom in his voice. "Make no mistake about it. I will not go to prison. Who do you think they'll believe an upstanding businessman with billions or an ex junkie prostitute? Don't force my hand. Now come on, let's have a little fun," he said, while walking away from her. She looked at him with cold fury in her eyes.

"Shaila, there are two Detectives here to see you," Sidney told her.

"Send them in." Shaila got up from her chair and greeted them at the door. "Detectives please have a seat." She motioned her hand to the couch. "What can I do for you?"

"I'm Detective Richards and this is my partner Detective Jacobs. We have a few questions about Miss Jones."

"Of course, but I already told the detective on the seen what happened. I will tell you everything I know. I want to know what happened to my friend."

"But we have to be thorough and go over every detail. You were the one who found Miss Jones in her apartment?" Detective Richards asked.

"Yes, my husband and I found her. I tried to revive her while my husband called 911. Detective, did Sara die of a drug overdose?

"Well, the autopsy report states there were no drugs on her system. So it would be safe to assume she didn't die of a drug overdose. Can you think of anyone who had a grudge against Miss Jones? Were there any jealous boyfriends or was he being stalked by anyone you could think of?"

"No, she never mentioned anybody bothering her."

"I have one last question for you Mrs. Anderson. Where were you between three and five pm last Friday?

"I was here until about four and then I went to Cancun for the weekend."

"Did you go by yourself?"

"No, I was with Marc Wilson the entire weekend."

"Thank you for your time. If you think of anything that might help us, please give us a call." He gave her his card."

"I will." She got up and walked them to the door.

"Going to Cancun with someone other than her husband. I wonder what that's all about," Jacobs commented.

"Well, as long as her alibi checks out, it's not our concern. Let's go."

Chapter 18

It was a cold rainy day in October, but that didn't deter anyone from coming to pay their respects to their friend and colleague. The funeral service was held in a large Methodist church, and the church was standing room only. The amount of people at her funeral just showed the love that people had for her. She was the sweetest, most hard working, and most loyal person Shaila had ever met. Shaila gave the eulogy. She was so distraught that she could barely get the words out. She spoke from her heart and soul about how beautiful she was. How she was loved by everyone and what a great attorney she would have been if her life wasn't cut short by her tragic death. She concluded her words of respect and love for Sara. The reverend led everyone in a word of prayer before the congregation was led to the burial site.

John and Shaila, Ben and his wife, and Luke and his wife were in the first limo followed by miles of cars being driven to the cemetery. Not a word was spoken in the limo. It didn't seem appropriate to say anything, Everyone was mourning and very sad. Shaila laid her head on John's shoulder for comfort.

They reached the cemetery. John got out of the limo, flared the umbrella, and helped Shaila out of the limo. They walked closely side by side to keep the rain at bay. After John and Shaila arrived at the burial site, she looked over to see Marc watching them. She gave him a smile and a nod. He smiled and nodded back to her. Sidney sang a beautiful rendition of Amazing Grace and Blessed Assurance, two of Sara's favorite hymns. A beautiful prayer was said and flowers were placed on her casket prior to the casket being lowered into the ground.

After the funeral, everyone made their way to Shaila and John's penthouse for a gathering. Shaila had managed to have a wonderful assortment of food. She had a fruit and vegetable plate, macaroni, potato salad, collard greens, fried chicken, corn on the cob, and an assortment of desserts and drinks. Everyone was eating, drinking, and laughing just the way Sara would have wanted. Playing on the HDTV screen was Sara at her birthday party. Everyone from the firm and all her closest friends were in attendance. John videotaped the entire party. It was a beautiful day and a wonderful memory. Everyone was drinking champagne, dancing, and just being silly cutting loose. Shaila looked at the video and remembered the fun they had that day. When she smiled, a lone tear fell down her face. John came over and asked if she was doing ok. She shook her head yes. And gave him a hug. Marc sat on the sidelines and glared at them with such venom that if looks could kill they both would be dead. Marc made his way over to where John and Shaila stood. Shaila looked up at him with a confused look in her eyes. She proceeded to introduce the two men.

"John, I'd like you to meet Marc Wilson. Marc, this is my husband, John."

They shook hands and both said it was a pleasure. They both had complimented each other on their accomplishments and made small talk. They talked about fishing, sports, and other stuff to pass the time. Shaila was very uneasy to say the least. She didn't want Marc to say anything about what happened between them before she had the chance to tell him the truth first. She gave Marc pleading looks trying to tell him not to tell him. He looked at her and winked. She made her way around like a gracious hostess. She talked to everyone and reminisced with her colleagues and friends. She refilled drinks and gathered dirty dishes. A few times she would turn to where Marc and John were and they would be deep in conversation. She prayed that Marc wouldn't tell John about their affair.

After what seemed like a lifetime, everyone finally began to make their exits. Shaila showed everyone out. The last person to leave was Marc. He said his goodbyes to Shaila and John by kissing Shaila on the cheek and shaking John's hand. After everyone had left, Shaila began to clean up. John grabbed her hand and said," baby, that can wait. Sit down and take a load off. I know you're exhausted. It's been a very long day, and you were the perfect hostess as always." He leaned his head down and gave a kiss.

"I think Sara would have approved. She wouldn't have wanted people to mourn her. She liked it when everyone was happy and everyone was. I also know she would have liked the food selection. She was more into soul food than I am." Shaila let out a soft chuckle. "God, I'm going to miss her."

"I know, me too. She was a really good person. We were lucky to have her in our lives," he replied.

John got up and started to clear the dishes and clean up. Shaila started to follow behind him to help. He quickly told her to sit back down. He would take care of the clean up. An hour passed and Shaila had changed into silk lounge pants and a spaghetti strap top. She walked downstairs to find John sitting on the couch drinking some brandy. He was relaxed with his shirt unbuttoned and his feet propped up on the coffee table. Shaila came around and stood in front of him. She straddled his legs and proceeded to sit down on the coffee table. He quickly removed his legs from the table and sat up. She looked into his eyes and asked, "where do we go from here?"

"I don't know. You tell me," he replied. "I do know I don't want to lose you, Shaila. I'm willing to do anything to work this out and keep you in my life."

"Before you say anything else, there's something I need to tell you." she said, closing her eyes.

"And I told you I don't want to know."

"You need to know."

He looked at her for a long pause. "Will it ruin the moment?"

"Yes," she said honestly.

"Can it wait? I don't want to hear any bad news right now."

"Ok, it'll keep."

The next day John and Shaila woke up in each other's arms. They had made their way up to the bedroom the night before and fell asleep. They woke up facing each other. They both smiled and kissed. That kiss led to another kiss making them want each other even more. John laid on top of her kissing down her neck into her cleavage. He took off her top and started sucking her nipples. She groaned in agreement to what he was doing. His kisses made his way down to her navel and around her lower stomach. He gently pulled her pants off and let them glide to the floor. He kissed down her leg and her feet. He began to undress himself. His erection stood on ceremony. He was ready for this. He had waited for so long for this moment. He didn't hesitate to enter her lovely temple. She exhaled a deep breath and matched him rhythm for rhythm. They made love for hours and finally after a totally exhausting workout they fell into each other's arms once again.

John woke up to an empty bed. He looked around, but there was no sign of Shaila. He put on his boxers and made his way downstairs to find Shaila sitting at the kitchen table.

"Shaila, are you ok?" He asked bewildered.

"John, I need to tell you something, and you may never forgive me, and it could be the end of our marriage." she let out a sigh.

He sat down next to her, but he didn't say anything because he already knew what she was going to tell him.

"Last weekend I went away to Cancun with Marc."

"Marc? Marc Wilson?"

"Yes."

"Umm, a business trip?" He hoped, but he knew it wasn't.

"No, it wasn't a business trip."

"You went away to Cancun with a person you just recently met?" He asked bewildered.

"No, Marc and I dated in college before I met you."

John rose up from the table and walked over to the window and stared out into the daylight. Shaila stayed seated and looked over in his direction. John turned back to her. "Why didn't you tell me you dated him? Were you hiding something?"

"No, she replied with a pleading voice. "It never came up. Marc and I were through when I met you."

"I just assumed when you first told me about this contract with Wilson Inc. you were meeting him for the first time. Why didn't you tell me then?"

"I didn't think it was important. You were the one I wanted. You're still the one I want. Marc and I were through. We had been for a long time."

"Why are you telling me this now?"

"John, I slept with him while we were in Cancun."

John turned and briskly walked out of the room. Shaila jumped from her chair and quickly followed him.

"John, wait."

He turned around and looked at her with tears welled in her eyes.

"I know this is a poor excuse, but I did it because I thought you cheated on me, and he made me feel wanted and loved. I'm not making excuses, but I felt so alone and needed someone, and he was there."

"But I didn't cheat on you, Shaila! I tried to explain that to you in the beginning, but you wouldn't listen!" He yelled, making her jump back.

"I know that now," she said, crying. "I'm sorry. I am so sorry. I love you, John."

"Jesus, Shaila, even though I didn't remember what happened that night, I knew in my heart I couldn't have sex with another woman. Yet, you knowingly have sex with another man, and not just any man, an ex-boyfriend." He turned and started up the stairs.

"Where are you going?" she asked.

"I can't talk to you right now. I'm going back to the hotel."

"Can't we talk about this?" She pleaded with him.

He looked at her and proceeded upstairs leaving her crying at the bottom of the steps.

Chapter 19

It had been a week since Shaila told John about her affair with Marc. He had barely spoken two words to her. She called him repeatedly and left messages, but he rarely returned her phone calls. Shaila sat at her desk looking out the picture window when Marc walked into her office.

"You've been avoiding me, why?"

She turned to face him. "I've been meaning to call you."

"Well, I've been here."

"I've been trying to figure out the right time to tell you John and I are trying to work things out."

"I see."

"I told John everything about Cancun, about us, everything," She said with sadness. He hasn't spoken to me since."

"He has no right to be upset with you after he slept with another woman first. He started this whole thing, remember? What a hypocrite. You're better off without him, Sha."

"That's where you're wrong. He didn't cheat on me. It was all a set up. She arranged the whole thing. My guess is she drugged him or something," she explained.

"Did he tell you that? Sha, don't you know he would say anything to get you to believe him?"

"I watched the disc over and over and he was passed out cold. He wasn't moving. He wasn't doing anything, but lying there. She was doing it all. She set him up. Don't you see? He never cheated on me. She wanted me think he did. Why? I don't know, but..." her voice faded. "He tried to tell me, but I wouldn't listen to him. I was the one who committed adultery, not him. So you see he has every right to be upset. I wouldn't blame him if he divorced me and never spoke to me again," she said through tears.

In the back of his mind he was hoping the same thing, but he kept a look of concern on his face.

"So, I guess that means there's no chance for us now, huh?" He asked.

"Marc, I'm sorry. I never should have let it go this far. Although the night we spent together was wonderful, it shouldn't have happened. I never meant to lead you on, and if I did, I'm sorry. That wasn't my intention. I have made a mess of everything. I never wanted to hurt you or John, but I have to try to make my marriage work. I hope you understand. Please understand."

"All I ever wanted was for you to be happy, and if John makes you happy, then as much as it breaks my heart, I'll just have to accept it and move on."

He got up from the chair, walked around to where Shaila stood, kissed her, turned and walked out the door.

Marc sat in his office with pure hatred in his eyes. His plan was going to hell and he was oblivious on how to stop it. He took another swig of his scotch and smashed the glass on his desktop breaking it into tiny pieces cutting his hand in the process. Cheryl walked into his office and saw the broken glass and his bleeding hand.

"What happened to you?" She asked.

He looked at her with so much hatred. It made a chill go straight through her.

"I'm going to have to take matters into my own hands," he replied.

"What does that mean?" she asked.

He got up from his desk, looked at her, and walked out of the office leaving her wondering what he meant.

Marc sat in his car he rented under an assumed name and watched as John came out of the elevator into the parking garage of the Carlton. John began walking over to his Mercedes. As soon as he was in clear view in front of Marc's car, he gunned it towards him. Before John could move out of the way, he had already been hit. The impact of the car threw John's body onto the windshield and Marc watched as his body rolled off the car onto the ground. Marc sped away without a second thought leaving John's limp body lying on the ground. People who saw what happened ran to his side to try and help.

Shaila was on her way to work when her cell phone rang.

"Shaila Andrson," she answered.

"Shaila, it's Jerry. You need to get to the hospital right now. John has been in an accident."

"Oh my God, is he…"

"No, but you really need to get here now," he said worriedly.

"I'm on my way," she replied, her hands shaking while holding the phone.

She called Ben to tell him what had happened and that she wouldn't be in. He told her to go handle business and to keep him posted. She headed to the hospital as fast as she could. When she got to the hospital, Jerry was waiting for her at the emergency room doors.

"John was hit by a car. Dr. Carter is with him."

"How bad is he?" She asked with worry.

"I don't know. I haven't spoken to Dr. Carter yet."

"Would you like me to call his parents?"

"Yes please."

"I'll be right back." He grabbed her hand and brought her into a hug. He came back to tell her that his parents were on their way. After what seemed like a lifetime, Dr. Carter came out to speak to them.

"Shaila, he has swelling in his brain and internal bleeding. The blunt trauma to his head caused the brain to swell."

"What does that mean?" She asked with concern.

"It means we're going to have to go in and relieve the pressure on his brain."

"And if you don't, he'll die?"

"It's a very strong possibility."

Shaila broke down and cried. Jerry held her to try and comfort her. "Do what you have to do. Please don't let him die, please," she pleaded with tears streaming down her face.

"I promise you Shaila, we will do everything we can to make sure that doesn't happen. We are trying to get him stabilized right now so we can go in and release the pressure."

"Can I see him?"

"Of course, but just to let you know, he's on a breathing machine. He's not alert.

"In other words, he's in a coma?"

"Yes."

She walked into the room and, sat down in the chair next to him. She grabbed his hand and prayed. "Please God bring my husband back to me. I have made a lot of mistakes, but please don't let John suffer for my indiscretions. Please don't let him die. He has a lot of family and friends who love him. He has too much good left to do here on earth. Please hear this prayer I'm sending your way. All I ask in your name, Amen.

As she put her head down, she felt someone touch her shoulder. She turned and saw John's parents standing behind her. She immediately got up and gave them a hug.

"How are you holding up, sweetheart?" Mrs. Anderson asked with concern.

"I'm ok. Have you spoken to Dr. Carter? Would you like me to have him paged?" She asked while walking hurriedly to the door.

"Calm down, sweetie. We spoke with Dr. Carter a few minutes ago. He gave us all the details."

"Ok, good. You know I just wish he would just wake up and tell me everything will be fine. I don't know what I will do if I lose him," she replied.

"Don't you dare think like that. I know in my heart he will pull through. Despite the problems you two are having, you two have incurred over the past few weeks, he loves you more than anything. He will not leave you. Just have faith in your husband and your love. You two have your whole life ahead of you. Give this to God and he will take care of the rest."

"Thanks, mom," she said while giving her a hug. "I'm going to give you two some time alone with John. I'm going down to the cafeteria and get some coffee.

"Sweetheart, you don't have to do that," Mrs. Anderson replied.

"No, it's ok, you sit with him for a while. I'm not going anymore. Can I bring you anything back?" She asked both of them.

"No, thank you," they both replied.

She kissed them both on the cheek and left the room.

Chapter 20

Shaila sat by John's side day in and day out after Dr. Carter went into his head and relieved the pressure on his brain. It was touch and go for a few minutes because his blood pressure dropped to a dramatic level, and they had a hard time stabilizing him, but after they go him stabilized, they were able to go back in and relieve the pressure and stop the internal bleeding. Shaila, his mother and father, Greg and Jasmine, and Tommy and his wife all sat vigil at his bedside. If they weren't in the room, they waited out in the waiting room. Shaila's mother and father would have been there as well, but they were on a cruise and they couldn't get back stateside, but they did send him well wishes and they called every chance they got. They said they would come see him as soon as they were back in town.

John was in a coma for four days, and if Shaila wasn't by his side, she would go into work, clear off her desk, and take any important clients. After she left work, she would go home, take a shower and head back to the hospital. There were many nights she would stay over night, but most nights, her mother-in-law made her go home and get some rest. "I will stay with him. I promise," her mother-in-law would tell her.

Shaila would read to him every night, and even though John was in a coma, Dr. Carter said he could still hear what was going on around him.

"John, I know you hear me. I wish you would open your eyes and talk to me. I miss you so much. Your patients miss you and need you. They've sent you cards, flowers, and gifts, and everyone's praying for you to open your eyes, and come back to us. Please just give me a sign you can hear me. I don't care what it is. Just let me know you hear what I'm saying to you," she pleaded kissing and carressing his hand. Much to her pleasure and surprise, she felt a light squeeze of her hand. She raised her head and looked at his hand squeeze hers. She didn't want to get her hopes up too much because he had done similar things in the past couple of days. Like the other day, his eyes fluttered like he was going to open them, but Dr. Carter said it was just a reflex action. Shaila called the nurses station anyway. Dr. Carter came into the room and examined him. This time it wasn't a false alarm. John actually opened his eyes and the first person he saw was Shaila. He looked at her and his eyes lit up with love. She immediately cried tears of joy and gave him the biggest hug she could muster without hurting him.

Dr. Carter ordered bloodwork, and a CT scan to see where his recovery stood. The nurse came in and took his blood and checked his temperature and his vitals. Dr. Carter sent the blood work to the lab and put a rush on the results.

While they waited for someone to come up and take him down for his CT, everyone was in his room waiting to see him, and were so ecstatic that he was awake. "Baby, thank God you're awake," his mother cried.

"It's good to see you, son," his father said with tears in his eyes. Shaila's brother's and their wives didn't come in, but they sent their well wishes from the waiting room.

It was that time. An orderly came into the room and said he was taking John down to CT. He went through the customary red rule, name and date of birth, and got John ready to wheel down to CT.

Before he could wheel him out, Shaila leaned down and kissed him. "Thank you for coming back to me. I love you so much."

John looked at her and said in a faint whisper and a smile, "I love you too." He squeezed her hand before they wheeled him out of the room.

John's recovery improved every day. He was out of the coma and Dr. Carter was able to drain the swelling from his brain with out any complications. His CT scan along with his bloodword all came back normal. His blood pressure was stable and he was getting stronger and stronger everyday. John and Shaila talked a lot while he was laid up in the hospital.

"Do you know how scared I was when I got the call you were hit by a car and that you might not make it? The thought of losing you scared me to death. You mean the world to me, and I know I don't have the right to ask for your forgiveness, but I am. I need you to forgive me." Tears welled up in her eyes. "What I did was wrong, and although I did it mostly because I was so sure you slept with another woman, that doesn't make it right. I love you, John. I love you so much, and I will do anything to rebuild your trust. I know it won't be easy, but I want the chance to try. Please give me that chance," she pleaded.

He stroked her hand and looked into her hazel eyes. "I love you, Shaila, and nothing will ever change that, but I don't know if I can get passed what happened between you and Marc. The thought of you making love to another man nearly killed me, but I'm willing to try. We've invested too much into our love to just throw it all away, but I can't automatically move back into the penthouse when I leave here. I think we should still live apart, and take things slow. It's going to take some time for me to trust you again. I'll find me a condo and live there for a while, and we can work on our marriage."

What he said broke her heart, but she understood. At least he didn't say no. There was hope they could rebuild what she broke. "That's all I'm asking. Thank you for giving me another chance. I love you, John. I really do."

Things were looking up for Shaila and John, but Marc was back to square one. With Shaila by John's side day in and day out, made Marc that much more resentful and determined. The police were investigating John's hit and run, but they weren't coming up with any tangible leads, and the investigation into Sara's death had run cold. Every lead they had came up was a dead end. Shaila and John's alibis were verified, and so were all the co workers and colleagues in the firm. They even checked out Marc's alibi, and since he was with Shaila in Cancun, he was ruled out. The only thing they could do for the time being was put the case on the back burner for now, but if there were any leads that developed, they would run those down.

Cheryl wanted to say something, but she was too scared. She was even more afraid of him now than ever before. She saw first hand what he was capable of. He killed Sara, that poor girl, and he had ran over another for getting in the way of what he wanted. What would he do to her if she were to betray him? She already knew the answer to that. He would kill her too. Even though she was scared to death, she had to do what was right. She couldn't let him keep hurting people, not anymore.

Shaila sat in her office going over some briefs when Ben walked in. "How's John doing?"

"He's doing much better, thank you for asking. He should be able to come home soon." He was going to recuperate at his parent's house for right now, but she didn't tell him that. "His Doctor's need to run a few more tests to be sure he's ready, but that's just a formality."

"That's great. Now how are you doing? Do you need anything?" He asked with concern.

"No, I'm good, but thanks for asking." She got up and gave Ben a hug when all of a sudden she fell dizzy and fell back in her chair.

"Are you ok?" He asked with concern.

"Yeah, I just got up too suddenly I guess. I haven't been eating that much lately either. I guess it's taking a toll on me."

"Listen to me. Go home and get some rest. With everything you have on your plate right now, you're running yourself ragged.

You need to relax. Now go home and get some rest. Whatever needs to be done here, I will take care of, go."

"Thank you, Ben. I'll see you tomorrow."

He winked at her. "Tell John Genie and I are praying for his speedy recovery." Genie was Ben's wife.

"Will do, thank you."

On the way home, Shaila stopped by the drugstore to pick up a pregnancy test. She was a week late and she was feeling nauseous and dizzy way too often. She knew what the results would be. She knew her body way too well. She was pregnant.

After waiting the appropriate amount of time after peeing on the stick, she looked at the results, and they were just as she expected. She was pregnant. Her face lit up with happiness and panic. With everything that was going on with her and John, this was going to be another factor they would have to consider. She walked over to her bed, picked up her cell phone, and immediately called her Obstetrician and set up an appointment.

John asked Shaila to go by his hotel and pick up a few things he needed to be more comfortable. She did as he asked and packed up his favorite robe, toothbrush, mouthwash, soap, and deodorant. She went into his closet and packed a few pairs of sweatpants and t-shirts. She walked over to the drawer and pulled out a few pairs of socks, boxer shorts, and threw them in the bag. She looked in the night stand to see if there was anything else he might need. She found a disc inside the drawer. She picked it up and stuck it in her purse. She wasn't sure why, but she had a feeling it was something important he might need. She packed his laptop along with his other things and headed back to the hospital.

Cheryl stood outside John's hospital room trying to conjure up the nerve to walk in when she saw Shaila walking towards her. She ducked around the corner out of Shaila's sight. Shaila walked into the room and made a beeline to John and gave him a long sensual kiss.

"Wow those are beautiful flowers." She walked over and smelled them. They were all over his room. "It looks like you've gotten more. Where did they all come from?"

"Some are from the hospital staff, and some were sent from your office. I don't know who sent the lavender roses. The card wasn't signed."

Shaila looked over at the beautiful bouquet of roses and a concerned look came over her face.

"What's the matter? Is something wrong?"

She looked over at him and pasted on a smile. "No, nothing's wrong. They're beautiful." She knew exactly who they were from, but she didn't want to rock the boat by telling him, and making him think about her and Marc's affair. They had been communicating better in the last few days, and she didn't want to mess that up. "I brought the things you asked for." She put the suitcase in the closet and brought his laptop over to him. She pulled the disc out of her purse and gave it to him. "I found this disc in your drawer. I thought you might need it for work."

"I forgot all about this. It was actually Sara's disc. I found it the day we found her in her apartment. It fell out of her jacket pocket when they were transporting her onto the gurney. I picked it up and put it in my pocket. Now, before you say anything about the law and tampering with evidence, I took it because I didn't want the police to find anything on that disc that would disparage her reputation. I was going to look at it first, and then give it to the police. I know it was stupid, but I wasn't thinking. Actually, I forgot I had it. With everything that was going on at the time, I completely forgot about it. It's probably some work from the office she brought to work from home. You sometimes bring work home."

"Yeah, I do, but I wasn't aware she was working on anything that she needed to work on from home. Let's take a look and see. You never know there could be something on there that might tell us what happened to her.

He popped the disc in this laptop, pushed a few keys, and an article popped on the screen.

"What's that?" She asked.

"It's some kind of a news article," he answered.

They both read the article.

"This can't be right," she said. "It says here Andrea and Kenneth Martin burned to death when their estate mysteriously caught fire and burned to the ground. The sole survivor was sixteen year old Andrew Martin who was not in the house when the blaze started. When the police asked the teenager where he was at the time of the fire, he said he was at a friend's house. Although his fingerprints were all over the gas can and lighter fluid, he seemed to have a solid alibi until the friend he said he was with didn't back up his story. The friend told the police Andrew wasn't with him that particular day, but he was with him the night before. Andrew Martin was convicted by a jury of his peers of two counts of first degree murder. He was sentenced to life without parole in prison." It also said, "the District attorney who tried the case, believed the inheritance was the motive he had for killing his parents. He stood to inherit over $100 million dollars upon their deaths. The bus that was transporting him to the prison facility had an accident and he escaped along with several other prisoners and disappeared."

"The picture in the article was a younger Marc Wilson. Marc had some corrective surgery to disguise his features throughout the years, but Shaila knew it was him. Marc was Andrew Martin, and he killed his parents."

"He showed up four years later at Yale University with the name of Marc Wilson as a transfer student. My God, I think I'm going to be sick," Shaila said. "I slept with a murderer, John." Then a realization came into her mind. "The whole time I've known him, he was a murderer. How could someone just up and murder their parents? There's something seriously wrong with this man, and I brought him into our lives. What the hell have I done?" She rose up from the chair and paced back and forth.

"Shaila, come on, sit down," he said, trying to calm her down.

She came over and sat down next to him, and he rubbed her back. She jerked around and looked at him. "Oh my God, John, what if he's the one who killed Sara? She obviously knew about his past because she copied it onto this disc. She was probably going to show it to me the day I went away to Cancun with him. He got to her before she could talk to me. That's the only explanation. She never really trusted him, and she told me that, but I shook it off because I dated him in college. God, I'm so stupid. I can't believe I didn't see this. I might have ruined my marriage for a murderer. He killed her and then whisked me off to Cancun." She began to cry.

"Shaila, please don't cry. You don't know that's what happened. It could have been a random attack."

"Given what we just found out, do you really think that's true? That wouldn't explain all the drugs all over her apartment. He staged it to look like a drug overdose. He didn't think they would do an autopsy. There were no drugs found in the system. He had to have done it. He killed her to keep his secret. That's the only logical explanation. She never did trust him, now I know why." She put her head on his shoulder and tears streamed down her face. "I feel so stupid."

"Shaila, don't blame yourself. He fooled a lot of people. It's not your fault, baby," he hugged her. "Baby, please don't cry."

She looked at him with horror on her face. "Oh my God, John, w-what if he's the one who ran you down?"

"Why would he run me down? I don't even know him."

"Because of his obsession with me. I told him you and I were trying to work things out, and that was right before you were hit by the car. He loves me. I love you. He thinks of you as a threat. He hates to lose. His only option is to kill you to have me for himself. I didn't think of it when he said it, but he said that he would always love me, nothing would keep us apart, and he would wait forever for me if he had to."

"Ok, say he's done all of these things, what do we do now? Should we go to the police?"

"No, we don't have any proof he killed her or ran you down."

"What about the disc? He was convicted of murder."

"Under the name of Andrew Martin, not Marc Wilson. It's all circumstantial. We need solid proof before we go to the police. If I can get his fingerprints, then I can give that to the police. They can scan it and it will come back to him being Andrew. That's my only shot."

"Why can't you let the police handle it? Why do you need to get involved?"

"Because he involved me by running you down and killing my best friend. This is personal. I'm going to make sure he goes down. He will not get away with this. If it means my life, he's going to pay for this."

"Whoa, Shaila, let's think about this. If he's as dangerous as I think he is, he will kill you. Please give this disc to the police and let them handle it. It's their job, Sha, please."

"If I go to the police, it will tip him off. I can't risk him coming here and finishing you off."

"You're not going to let this go, are you?" He started to get ot of bed, but Shaila stopped him.

"Whoa, where do you think you're going?"

"With you, I'm not about to let you go by yourself.

"You can't. You're not well enough. Stay here. All I'm going to do is go see him and get something that has his fingerprint on it and take it back to Detective Richards along with the disc. He won't suspect anything of it. He wants me with him. I'll make him think I'm confused and I don't know what I want. I'll be back I promise." She kissed him and ran out of the room with him yelling behind her.

"Sha, goddammit wait!"

Chapter 21

Shaila walked into her penthouse to change her clothes. She wasn't sure what she was going to do yet, but she had to do something. She had to get proof of who Marc was. She knew Marc killed Sara, and he was responsible for trying to kill John. She was headed out the door when she found a nice looking young lady standing in the doorway.

"May I help you?"

"Yes," the young woman answered.

"Have we met?" Shaila asked. "Wait, I know you. You're the woman on the disc. I know you're the one who set up my husband. I just don't know why, but right now I have more important business I need to attend to. I'll deal with you later. Now get the hell out of my way before I move you the hell out of my way."

"Wait, please," Cheryl pleaded. "I know who ran your husband down, and who killed Sara."

Shaila looked at her with fury in her face. "What do you know?"

"Everything."

They both went inside the penthouse. Cheryl told Shaila everything. She told her about Boston, about Sara and John. She even mentioned Marc's parents, and how they died.

"My God, what kind of monster is he? Why didn't you go to the police after you found out he killed Sara?"

"He said he would kill me. You have to believe me. I never took part in Sara's murder. I didn't even know about her until I saw the story on the news and he told what he did. I was just supposed to go to Boston, seduce John, and tape us having sex. The only problem was John didn't want me. He was adamant about his love for you." Shaila's heart skipped a beat with her words. "I had to drug him and make it look like we had sex. He was passed out cold. I put some of my sleeping pills in his drink. Marc told me to do whatever I needed to do to get the disc made. I'm so sorry, Shaila."

"Why did he do this?"

"He wants you. You're his obsession."

"All of this because I broke up with him more then ten years ago?"

Cheryl nodded yes. "He's always been obsessed with you."

"Where is he now?" Shaila asked.

"He's probably at the office. I haven't spoken to him all day. I want to help. I have to find a way to make my part in this right. Please tell me what I can do. I know I can't take back what happened to you and John, but I can help put Marc away for a long time. What do you say?"

"How do I know you won't go running back to Marc with information."

"Because I give you my word I won't."

"Well, excuse me for my rudeness, but your word doesn't mean shit to me."

"I deserved that."

"I guess you do," Shaila said with sarcasm.

"I just want to help, no strings attached. I never signed on to be an accomplice to murder."

She reluctantly relented. "Alright, but if you tip him off, God's wrath has nothing on me."

Shaila and Cheryl arrived at Marc's office building where they saw his Maserati parked in the designated parking spot. Cheryl motioned to his Maserati. "He's here. What's the plan?

"I don't know. I was just going to play it by ear. I figured I would turn my cell phone video on and get him to say something incriminating. The only problem is how do I do that without tipping him off."

"Let me do it. He won't suspect anything because in his mind if he goes down, I go down."

"No, Cheryl, it's too dangerous, and I can't say I honestly trust you either."

"I don't see where we have any other choices here. If you go in asking questions, you'll tip him off for sure. Let me do this. Let me please try and make things right."

"I don't know. I don't feel right about this. Maybe we should just go to the police, and let them handle it."

"If we go to the police, they will bring him in for questioning, and if they don't have enough evidence to hold him, he will be back on the street and mad as hell. You've seen what he's capable of. He will kill John and then me." Cheryl took out her cell phone, and turned on record and put it in her back pocket. "Stay here. I'll be right back."

"Cheryl," Shaila hesitated. "Be careful."

Cheryl gave her a curt nod, got out of the SUV, and walked into the building. As Shaila sat in her SUV, her cell rang.

"Hello."

"Thank God. Where are you? I was on the verge of calling Detective Jacobs to go and look for you." John said with concern in his tone.

"Please don't do that. I'm ok, don't worry. We're handling it."

"What do you mean we? Who's there with you? Where are you?"

"Baby, please don't worry. I love you. I'll come by later."

Before he could say anything else, she hung up.

Cheryl checked her phone before she walked into Marc's office. "Here we go,"

"Cheryl, what are you doing here?" Marc asked.

"Marc, I'm scared."

"Cheryl, everything will be fine, The police don't suspect a thing. As a matter of fact, the case has gone cold. They don't have any leads, so stop worrying."

"I don't understand why you ran John down in that car. Was he really that much of a threat?"

"Yes, he was, and he still is. The bastard should be dead. That's the universe fucking with me, With him alive, I will never have Shaila back."

"Weren't you afraid someone would see you run him down in the parking garage? You took a big gamble running him down in broad daylight."

"No one was around to see me ok? Why are you asking me so many questions?"

"I'm just scared, that's all. I just think you've gone too far this time."

"Are you planning on going to the police?"

"No, of course not, I'm just as deep in this as you are. I'm sure you'll make sure I go down too. I'm not about to dig my own grave."

He looked at her skeptically, and that made her even more nervous, but she had a job to do and she was damn sure going to do it. "What's wrong with you, Cheryl. You seem on edge."

"Well, I also read they did an autopsy on Sara's body. I thought you said they would just rule it a drug overdose. Now they know there were drugs in her system. Won't they rule it a homicide? They'll have to investigate."

"Yeah, that was unfortunate, I misjudged that one. The police aren't as dumb as I thought, but they don't have any evidence I did anything. There's no fingerprints or anything else that could implicate me, so relax, will you? You're going to give yourself a coronary. Now go home, draw yourself a nice bubble bath, have a drink, and relax."

"You're right. I think I will. I just need to relax." She let out a deep breath and said, "thanks, I feel better now."

"Good, go home."

She turned and walked out the door. She grinned a wicked smile and practically ran to the elevator. She checked her phone to make sure she got everything recorded, and she was thrilled when she got their entire conversation recorded on her phone.

Shaila watched as Cheryl came out of the with a smile on her face. Cheryl climbed in the passenger seat and said, "I got him." She showed Shaila her phone and played a little of their conversation.
"Did he suspect anything?"
"Not a thing, he sang like a canary."
"Yes!" Shaila said with excitement. "Let's take this over to Detective Jacobs. We've got him now," Shaila said.
Marc just happened to be looking out the window when he saw Cheryl get into Shaila's SUV. Why was Cheryl getting into Shaila's SUV, and why didn't Shaila come up? Why was Shaila asking so many questions? All of those questions swam around in his head. What did Cheryl do? Marc picked up his keys and rushed out of his office. He took his private elevator down to the lobby, and rushed through the lobby and out the doors to his Maserati, but before he could make it to his Maserati, he noticed Cheryl and Shaila sitting in Shaila's SUV. They were too preoccupied to see him, so he ducked behind a tree. He did see Cheryl pull out her phone and hand it to Shaila. He began to panic. Sweat beaded up on his forehead and his heart began racing uncontrollably. Shaila started to drive away. Once they were out of sight, he ran to his Maserati hoping they weren't too far ahead for him to catch up and follow them. Luckily, they were stopped by a stop light. Marc followed far enough behind them that they couldn't see him. After about a twenty minute drive, Shaila pulled into the one place he didn't want her to pull into, The New York police department. Shaila and Cheryl got out and walked into the police station together. Marc immediately drove away in a panic.
Cheryl and Shaila walked up to the officer at the front desk and asked to speak with Detective Richards or Jacobs. Detective Jacobs walked out to greet them, and Cheryl couldn't take her eyes off the

gorgeous Detective. "Jesus, that man is fine," Cheryl whispered into Shaila's ear.

Shaila smirked. "He is fine."

"Fine doesn't do him justice. He is the finest white man I've ever seen."

Cheryl, you might want to close your mouth. You're dooling."

"Hello ladies, you wanted to see me?"

"We have something you will want to hear," Shaila said."

"Follow me." They followed him to an interview room for privacy. "What can I do for you?"

Cheryl gave him her phone and he pressed play on the recording. He listened to the recording in its entirety. After he listened, he shut it off. "How did you get this?" He asked, looking at Shaila.

Cheryl and Shaila looked at each other. "Cheryl recorded their conversation about twenty minutes ago. Shaila pulled out the disc and gave it to him. "This is why Sara was killed. She knew Marc's secret. Marc Wilson is Andrew Martin. He was convicted of killing his parents when he was sixteen. He escaped and disappeared. He showed up four years later as Marc Wilson. He killed Sara, and ran down John."

He shook his head in anger. Who do you think you are, Charlie's Angels? You should have come to me the minute you suspected anything. That's my job, not yours. You two could have been hurt, maybe even killed. Did he suspect anything?"

"No, we're not that stupid to get caught." Cheryl said with sarcasm. "What happens now?"

"Well, we will bring him in for questioning." He looked over to Shaila, but you know how this works. This recording is good, but it probably won't hold up in court, but with this recording, we can put some heat on him and maybe he'll slip up. You two go home, and let us handle it. I'll let you know what happens."

Shaila dropped Cheryl off at her car and drove to the hospital to see John. As soon as Shaila walked in his room, John said, "where the hell have you been? I've been blowing your cell phone up trying to reach you. Why didn't you answer?"

"Baby, would you calm down? First of all, Cheryl and I got a recorded conversation of Marc confessing to everything. He confessed to your hit and run and to killing Sara we took the recording to Detective Jacobs. Second, the reason you couldn't reach me was because I turned my phone off. I knew you would try calling me to change my mind, and third, we were in no danger. Marc didn't suspect a thing. Now are you happy?"

"I'm happy you're still alive and well, but I'm not happy you went out and played Cagney and Lacy. You are so stubborn. And when the hell did Cheryl come into all of this? What does Cheryl have to do with any of this?"

"Well, she came to the penthouse today and explained everything to me. Marc made her go to Boston and seduce you. She was to get you into bed and videotape the two of you having sex and send it to me. The first time she came to your room, you turned her down. That's when she drugged you the second time. She took your clothes off, undressed herself, got on top of you, pressed record, and voila the two of you were having sex on tape, but you didn't know that.

"Why go through all of that? What did she have to gain? Was it all about the money?"

"No, Marc pretty much forced her to do it. He told her he would cut her off if she didn't do it. Everything she has Marc gave her. Her condo, her car, clothes everything, but at first, she was supposed to seduce you. I was supposed to find out, and leave you. She had nothing to do with Sara or you. She didn't find out about you and Sara until after the fact. That's why she came to me in the first place. She felt horrible and wanted to make things right, and get Marc. She didn't know he had killed Sara or about you. She was actually the one who got Marc on the recording."

"So Marc set this whole thing up? Well, I don't have to ask why. I've already figured that much out."

"Baby, I am so sorry I got us into this mess. I had no idea what he was capable of. I never thought in my wildest dreams he would be capable of murder, or any of this. I just thank God he didn't kill you."

"I guess by getting rid of me he would have a clear path to you."

"Can you ever forgive me for what I did?" She asked with tears in her eyes. She put her head down on his hands and started to cry harder. He stroked her hair and lifted her chin to meet his gaze.

"I'm willing to try if you are. We have a lot to work out, but I love you, and I want this to work," he said with a smile.

"I'm willing to do anything to work this out. I love you so much, baby. You have no idea how much. You won't regret this. I promise." She put her head on his chest and closed her eyes. She just had to deal with one more matter. Whose baby was she carrying?

Chapter 22

Cheryl walked into her condo and turned on the lights. She threw her keys on the key tray and walked into the kitchen. She pulled a bottled water from the refrigerator and took a drink. She walked into her bedroom and before she could get all the way inside, she was grabbed from behind and hit in the back of her head. She woke up with a severe headache and blurred vision. She felt a burning sensation on her wrists and ankles. Her hands were tied behind her back and her ankles were tied together. She had tape over her mouth to keep her from screaming. It took her some time to figure out where she was. She looked around the room and didn't see anyone, but heard footsteps coming down the hall towards her bedroom. She squirmed to try to get free in a panic, but she couldn't get free.

"I see my little angel is awake."

She looked in front of her with complete surprise to find Marc sitting on her bed. He had a gun in one hand and a sandwich in the other.

"Where are my manners? Would you like a bite? It's your favorite, ham and cheese."

She tried to say something, but the tape over her mouth forbade her to.

"What, are you trying to tell me something? I'm going to take this tape, but if you scream, I will hurt you, but I don't want to do that. So keep your mouth shut."

She nodded, and he took the tape off. She licked her lips and around her mouth to get her feeling back. "Marc, what are you doing? Why do you have me tied up? And why do you have a gun on me?"

"Why were you asking me so many questions at my office?"

"I already explained that to you. I'm scared, that's all. I needed reassurance."

"Wrong answer. Let's try this again. Why did you leave with Shaila and go to the police station?"

Her throat went dry, and her heart sank into her stomach. She knew she was busted. She looked up at him with fear in her eyes. What was he going to do next? Was he going to kill her? Torture her, what?

"Why did you sell me out?"

"I couldn't take the guilt anymore. Too many people are dead. I couldn't have that on my conscience."

"You do realize you'll have to pay for what you've done.'

"So be it, go ahead and kill me. I don't care what you do. I'm probably going to go to prison anyway. I'm an accessory to murder after the fact. Do whatever the hell you want."

He picked up a knife he had on the bed beside him and moved toward her. She thought he was going to stab her to death with her own kitchen knife. She shut her eyes and accepted her fate. He walked behind her and cut the ropes tying her hands together. He walked in front of her and cut her ankle free. "Get up."

She was confused, but she did what she was told. She looked into his eyes and saw pure evil. "Where are we going?"

He had the gun pressed up against her back while inside his coat pocket. They walked from her apartment to her car. He told her to get in and drive. She asked again where they were going, He said nothing. He just told her when and where to turn. She followed his directions. She realized where he was taking her, and she suddenly became very scared.

"Please, whatever it is you're going to do, don't," she pleaded with him.

He looked at her with cold green eyes, which made her jerk with fear.

John was in his hospital bed half asleep when Detective Jacobs walked in. "Detective, what can I do for you?

"Hi, Mr. Anderson, how are you feeling?"

"I'm doing much better, thank you. Is everything ok?"

"Well, I was looking for your wife." He answered with concern in his voice.

"She went home for the night. Why? Is everything ok?"

"It might be nothing."

"What do you mean? Is Shaila in danger?'

"We don't know. We went to Marc's house to ask him some questions about Sara's murder and your hit and run, but when we got there the place was ransacked and empty. Some of his clothes were gone and the safe was empty. It looks like he left in a hurry."

"My God! Do you think he knows you guys are onto him?" He asked in complete panic.

"He might."

"What are you doing to keep Shaila safe?"

"I've already sent a squad car to your house. Don't worry, I'll make sure Shaila's safe.

John began to get out of bed so he could go and make sure Shaila was safe. He was in a complete panic. He had never felt this scared about anything in his life. He didn't know how, but he had to get to Shaila, and make sure she was all right. Detective Jacobs stopped him and made him get back into bed.

"I will handle this. You're in no condition to go anywhere. You're still very weak. Let me do my job. I promise you Shaila will not be harmed." He turned around and walked out the door.

Shortly after Detective Jacobs left, John got out of bed and hobbled his way over to the closet. He put on a pair of sweatpants, a t-shirt, and tennis shoes. He made his way to the elevator without being seen.

Shaila walked into her penthouse and put her keys on the key hook. She was exhausted. All she really wanted to do was lie down and get some sleep. She went into the den and sat down on the sofa. She patted her stomach and laid her head back on the couch. She was feeling better about her and John, but she didn't tell him about the baby. She was almost positive it would prove to be Johns because she and Marc used a condom. Little did she know the condom broke and Marc didn't tell her. She wanted to tell John about the baby, but one, she hadn't seen her OB yet to confirm and two, she didn't want John to have any doubts who the baby really belonged to. Her stomach started to growl. She realized with everything that happened that day, she hadn't eaten anything.

She made her way to the kitchen to make her a sandwich. She took the turkey breast, cheese, and mayo out of the refrigerator and placed it on the counter. She turned to walk over to the pantry to get the bread when she heard a noise. She quickly turned towards the noise, dropping the bread on the floor. "Who's there?" She panicked. There was no answer. That didn't satisfy her, so she took a knife from the knife block and lurked around the doorways and corners. She checked out the laundry room, the den, and the dining room, but saw nothing. She began to walk up the stairs when she heard the floor creek. She immediately turned around to find Marc with a gun to Cheryl's head.

"Cheryl, are you alright? Shaila asked.

She shook her head no.

"Drop the knife, Shaila," Marc demanded.

She dropped the knife on the floor. "Marc, put the gun down, please. We can talk about this."

"What's there to talk about? What's done is done. Can't change it."

"I can help you," Shaila pleaded.

"Humph! You can help me?" He took the gun from Cheryl's head and pointed it at Shaila. He waved the gun towards the den. The three of them walked into the den. Cheryl and Shaila sat on the couch while Marc sat in the chair across from them with the gun still pointed at them. He turned to Shaila. "Can't you see I did all of this for you? You and I were supposed to be married. We were supposed to have children together, not you and John. John never deserved your love. I did!" He said with a volume that caused the two of them to jump.

"I understand how you feel. I hurt you so badly. You're right. You're the one I should have married." She tried to use psychology on him to try to bring his guard down. "I realize John and I don't belong together, You're the one I want. I'll divorce John so you and I can be together."

"You'd do that for me?"

"Of course, but you're going to have to do something for me though."

"What?"

"Let Cheryl go. We can't start our new life together with her here. Don't you want to be alone with me?"

"Of course I do, but what if she goes to the police?"

"She won't. Will you, Cheryl?"

"No, I won't go to the police."

"You two went to the police earlier today, why?"

"I made Cheryl go with me to the police station. I was scared. I didn't know what to do. I thought you would hurt me too."

He turned away from them and walked to the window and looked out.

"What are you doing?" Cheryl whispered to Shaila.

"Sssh, I know what I'm doing."

Marc turned back around and walked back to them. "I can't believe you would think I would hurt you. I love you, Shaila. I'd never hurt you."

"I know that now. I'm sorry I went to the police. Please forgive me."

Just as Marc was going to reply to what Shaila had said to him, the phone rang. Shaila looked over to the phone then looked back at Marc.

"Answer it."

"Hello," Shaila answered.

"Shaila, it's Detective Jacobs, are you ok?"

"Mom, hi how are you?"

"Is Marc there with you?"

"Yes, I miss you too, I can't wait to see you."

"Is Cheryl with you?"

"Yes, I look forward to you coming to New York and visiting. It has been so long since I have seen you. I miss you and daddy so much."

"Shaila, just listen to me. Stay calm. We have cops surrounding your building. Try to keep him calm, ok?"

"Ok, listen mom, can I call you back later? I have to prepare for court tomorrow morning, I have a lot of work to get done."

Jacobs hung up the phone. Shaila continued to talk like she was talking to her mother. She didn't want Marc to get suspicious. She said I love you and hung up the phone.

"Your parents are coming for a visit?" Marc asked.

"Yes, they are."

"That's nice. I can't wait to see them again."

"I can't wait for you to see them again."

"Why didn't you mention we were together?"

"I wanted to surprise them when they came out. I'm sorry. I didn't mean to hurt your feelings. I should have told her. I'm sorry."

"It's ok. You're right. Let's surprise them," he said with a smile on his face.

When Marc wasn't paying attention to them, she told Cheryl in a whisper, "Detective Jacobs has the building surrounded. He said to try to keep Marc calm."

Cheryl nodded her head in agreement to what Shaila had said.

"What are you two talking about over there?" Marc asked with suspicion.

"I was just telling Cheryl how I couldn't wait for you and I to start our new life together."

He looked from Shaila to Cheryl and back to Shaila. He just happened to see a glimpse of a cop run past the window when he turned around. He yelled in a fit of rage and fiercely closed the curtains. "Do you think I'm stupid?!" He yelled. "Who were you talking to on the phone?"

"My mother."

"Don't lie to me! You were talking to the cops weren't you?"

"No I wasn't."

"Stop lying to me!" He started throwing things in a fit of rage.

Cheryl and Shaila began to panic. Shaila was trying to keep Marc calm, but she couldn't get through to him.

"All I did was love you, and you do this to me!" He looked in Shaila's direction.

He turned towards Cheryl. "Get up!" He waved the gun at her. "Get over there!" Cheryl got up and walked over to the wall where Marc was pointing the gun. Tears streamed down her face. She was terrified. She knew Marc was going to kill her. He looked over in Shaila's direction and said, "you just killed her."

Marc turned to face Cheryl and put the gun up to her head. With his finger on the trigger. He began to squeeze. When all of a sudden Shaila came from behind him and tackled him into the wall. They struggled with the gun. The gun flew free and landed on the floor across the room. Cheryl immediately went after the gun. Marc followed her with his eyes. Although Shaila got a few good jabs and kicks in, she couldn't overpower him. He punched her in the face and she immediately fell to the floor. He ran over to Cheryl and as she was about to turn the gun on him, he grabbed it and wrestled it away from her. He hit her in the face with the gun, and she fell to the floor. He turned the gun on Cheryl and two shots rang out. Shaila screamed. Blood splattered all over Cheryl's face as Marc's body fell to the floor beside her. Cheryl and Shaila looked over to the door to find John standing there with his glock in his hand. John had killed Marc to save Cheryl's life. All of a sudden the police busted in the front door, with their guns drawn. Jacobs assessed the situation and took the gun from John's hand. He went over to where Marc's body laid and determined he was dead. He called in the forensics and declared Anderson's home a crime scene. Shaila ran to her husband and hugged him as tightly as she could. They see Cheryl standing against the wall not far from Marc's body. Shaila walked over to her and gave her a hug and asked her if she was ok. Tears streamed down their faces. Cheryl said she was ok and hugged Shaila back. She thanked her for saving her life. She walked over to John, hugged, and kissed him on his cheek. She looked up at him, and began to say thank you, but he put his hands up to her mouth and said, "you're welcome."

Epilogue

"Hush little baby don't say a word," Shaila began to sing to Christina Marie while sitting in the rocking chair in the nursery. She looked up to see John standing in the doorway smiling from ear to ear. Shaila smiled back at me. "Do you know how happy I am right now?" She asked.

"Well, I have an idea, but why don't you tell me anyway. It gives me an ego boost."

"I'm the luckiest woman alive to have a loving, attentive husband and the most beautiful baby girl anyone has ever seen. She looks just like her daddy."

"She does, doesn't she? She has my eyes, and your smile," John said.

"The past year and a half took a lot of hard work and prayer, but it got us back to where we were before the mess with Marc. I'm just glad you didn't give up on me, on us. Although it would have killed me, I wouldn't have blamed you if you walked away, and never looked back. If it's any consolation, I always knew in my heart this baby was yours. I didn't need a DNA test to tell me what I already knew, but I knew you would always wonder in the back of your mind if Chrissie really was your baby. We all needed to know, if anything, to have closure."

"That's all in the past, baby. Chrissie is our baby. Marc is dead and buried, and he will never hurt you or anyone else again. We are together and nothing will ever tear us apart. You two are the love of my life. I would move heaven and earth to make sure no harm came your way." He pointed to Shaila then to Chrissie.

Shaila got up with the baby in her arms and moved over to John and gave him a kiss. The three of them stood together in a warm embrace. John leaned down and gave little Chrissie a kiss on her cheek. He looked up at Shaila and said, "I love you, Shaila."

"I love you, too, John."

"Oh honey, would you look at that? Someone left the most beautiful bouquet of sterling silver roses in that SUV. It must be a very special occasion. Someone will be surprised all right."

"With roses like that, someone will be more than surprised. They'll probably be out right astonished."

The older couple walked from the parking garage to their penthouse apartment.

About the Author

Kristin Glenn was born in Seymour, Indiana in 1973. She graduated from Seymour High School in 1992. After high school she attended Indiana State University where she met her future husband, Walt. After living in Seymour close to her parents and her two brothers, she married and moved to Indianapolis with her incredible husband and their three handsome sons.